IDOLATRY

A Story in Five Parts

The fiction of Quent Cordair
resides at

As It Should Be

quentcordair.com

Also by Quent Cordair

A Prelude to Pleasure

The Lunch Break Collection

The Match

The Seduction of Santi Banesh

At Home with Heather James

Sheltered

Mujahid

IDOLATRY

A Story in Five Parts

Part I

Genesis

by

Quent Cordair

Cordair Inc.

Napa   MMXIV

Published by
Cordair Inc.
1301 First St., Napa, CA 94559
(707) 255-2242
www.cordair.com

This book contains an excerpt from the forthcoming title *A New Eden*, Part II of *Idolatry*, by Quent Cordair. This excerpt has been set for this edition only and may not reflect the final content of the forthcoming edition. Excerpt from *A New Eden* copyright © 2014 by Quent Cordair.

To my wife and best friend,

Linda,

who makes it possible.

With deepest gratitude to

Ayn Rand,

for being, thinking, showing.

Part I

Genesis

One

THE BOY WAS STANDING on the summit of the hill above
her, the spring grasses waving at his feet, his white tunic
carving clean against the azure sky. He was waiting for her,
hands on his hips, smiling his irresistible smile. She ran up
the hill to join him, her feet barely touching the ground.

Whether she had fallen or knelt when she reached
him, she neither knew nor cared—the musky scent of
his sandal leather mingled with the pungency of the earth
between her fingers and the sweetness of wildflowers
twining through her hair. She lifted her eyes to follow the
arching line between his bare shin and supple calf, the
skin as smooth as polished marble. A soft wind pressed
the folds of his tunic against his thighs, hollowing a vale
between them. His hands were asking for hers—her fingers
were found and encircled by the warmth of his own. She
hadn't realized how cold hers had been. From her knees,
she studied the knot of his belt until, as he raised her to
her feet, her gaze was drawn upwards to his chest, to his
lips, into his eyes—eyes that were shining orbs of hazel
agate flecked with umber and gold, rimmed in moss green.
Her gaze flitted from one iris to the other, marveling at the

minute differences between them, delighting in the detail, while his eyes studied her own, penetrating more deeply—

"*Sira . . .*"

Her name came on the breeze dancing through his bronze curls, a dark-flamed corona pierced through with brilliant rays from above.

"*Sira . . .*"

She was too close to his lips—she didn't dare look at his lips, though the heat of his breath was between her own. She gasped as he lifted her into his arms and began to spin her slowly around, and as the heavens turned above his head, she fell deeper and deeper into eyes from which she could conceal nothing, wanted to conceal nothing. He was breaking through every barrier within her and soon would know everything—

"*Siranush!*" Her mother's voice snapped her back into the present.

The cacophony of the bazaar rose in Sira's ears, the babel of voices climbing and tumbling, the clangor of copper pots and bronze ware, the clinking of silver coin. From the street came the bleating of goats and sheep, the crack of the crop against an oxen's dusty flank, the grind of wooden wheels on paving stones.

She blinked and regarded the length of fine white wool in her hands: it was the same swath of fabric she had been folding when left in charge of their stall by her mother, now returning, with her basket filled with fresh chickpeas, ripened olives, dried apricots, mint sprigs and flatbread.

"Less dreaming, Sira. More selling."

Sira sighed and pressed her nose into the piece of bread her mother had torn off for her, still warm from the oven. The figs and cheeses of the farmer in the stall adjacent were beginning to tempt—either would be good with the bread, both would be better. She tried not to look at them. From the stall opposite, the fat Phoenician who sold donkey saddles was still leering lasciviously, while his wife, not more than a teenager herself, glared daggers at the younger girl from around the edges of her veil. Sira closed her eyes. The vision of her lovely young god had slipped away like a startled stag into the forest.

She scanned the heads of the crowd in the bazaar, searching for the boy's curls—but today, he was nowhere to be seen.

Checking her reflection in the polished bronze hanging from the tent pole, she tucked an unruly wisp beneath her plaited braids and adjusted her ivory hairpin. With eyes as large as dates, their irises as dark and richly shining as her hair and lashes, she had learned to use her other gifts judiciously. A mere hint of her smile was usually more than sufficient to secure all the attention she might desire, and often, unfortunately, more.

That morning she had donned her coral-colored tunica and belted it with her favorite sash, a brilliant blue silk from the distant East, trimmed in gold brocade and embellished with six pairs of finely embroidered birds that flitted and played across the blue silk sky. While her family was far from wealthy—over the years, privation had too often been the unwelcome guest at mealtimes—Sira had always been allowed to select her apparel and accessories from the best of their inventory: the better she looked, the more she sold, and today, she had never looked better.

She could feel no guilt over the daydream. That morning she had already sold more fabric and cookware than the rest of her family had sold the whole of the week before. Her brother had disappeared again, to gamble with the boys in the alley; her father was likely sitting under a tree or leaning against a wall somewhere, exchanging news and gossip or bartering with the craftsmen and other traders for new stock. It mattered little to him what the goods were, as long as they were of good quality and saleable at a profit down the road. Every few days or weeks the family would break down their tent, pack up their wagon and join another caravan, to travel the old Roman roads to the next town that would accept them. From Constantinople to Antioch, from Ephesus to Neocaesaria, in towns large and small across the breadth of the Eastern Empire, Sira had sold kitchen utensils, aphrodisiacs, buttons, brooches, goats, carved wooden boxes, spices, honey, scented oils and ceramic pots. She hated selling dried fish. She loved selling textiles, clothing and jewelry. The trove of fine silk her father had acquired for a pittance from a cash-strapped Sogdian trader was a rare treat, by far the best fabric yet to pass through her hands. Her enthusiasm for the luxurious textures and rich colors was infectious to prospective buyers.

Or to most of them. Yesterday, she had been attempting to accommodate a fussy man who was flipping through her fabrics dismissively, disheveling her carefully folded stacks, mussing the samples hung neatly from the cross poles, complaining that nothing was quite the right hue and finding flaws and imperfections invisible to mere mortals. She had been on the verge of asking him if his mother had had the same keen eye, and if so, why she hadn't traded him away as a child to the slavers for a couple of chickens, all things considered, when she glanced up to see—the boy.

He was standing in the middle of the street, staring at her intently, looking as if he had just found something he hadn't realized he had lost. Pedestrians detoured around him. Cart drivers cursed him. How long he had been standing there watching her she didn't know. Casually, she brushed her fingers through her hair: the fresh white lily she had tucked there that morning was still in place.

By the time the fussy man had moved along to be disappointed by the farmer's fruits and cheeses, the boy was walking away, nearly out of sight.

Sira had thrown a quick excuse to her mother and followed him.

She trailed him through the bazaar and beyond, into the town's central square, in the middle of which was an elaborately carved marble fountain. As the boy passed it, he touched his fingers to his lips and raised his hand in a saluting kiss.

Sira hadn't ventured as far as the square before, her family having arrived in town only a few days earlier. As she neared the fountain, she found herself slowing.

It was hardly the largest or most ornate fountain she had ever seen, and she had seen many in her travels, yet the more closely she approached, the more captivated she became. Its lower tier was composed of four remarkably lifelike elephants, facing the four winds, water spouting from their trunks, each creature captured in its own motion and mood. The southerly elephant was stomping in agitation, trunk cocked high and to the side. The easterly animal was bracing defiantly, head lowered and ears back, trunk pointing outwards. She circled to the northerly creature, who bore its burden with resignation, its trunk swinging low. The westerly elephant was the youngest of the four; it seemed eager to trot away at the first excuse, ears perked and flapping happily. She thought the elephants magnificent. She wanted to name them all and feed them and ride the youngest to the sea, where they would sit together in the sand and eat pistachios and watch the waves for hours on end.

The elephants were positioned between four columns, each of which was exotically adorned with bundles of reeds, Egyptian motifs, and capitals of palm fronds. A herd of small antelope peered out from around the columns. Some nibbled on the reeds; others drank from the fountain's pool. The elephants and columns supported a wide, spouted bowl, around the rim of which lounged the figures of three graceful girls of about Sira's age: one lay prone, her chin resting on her clasped hands as she admired her own reflection in the water below; another was supine, her leg bent and raised at the knee, her arm hanging loosely off the side of the bowl's rim, her face to the sun; the third was sitting with her knees drawn to her chest as she contemplated the fountain's central figure, which stood majestically on a stepped circular dais rising out of the upper pool.

The rendering of the elephants, the antelope, and the three girls was so masterful as to be nearly beyond Sira's ability to grasp or accept. Surely these living, breathing beings had been turned to stone in an instant by the Gorgons and they would spring to life again the moment the spell was broken. But when her gaze had risen to the top tier, she felt as if she herself might have come under the Gorgons' spell: her feet were rooted to the spot where she stood. She couldn't take her eyes off of the figure of the woman above.

At any moment, the woman's name or title would spring to mind. Sira was certain she recognized her—yet, she couldn't remember. . . . She was a great queen, or the wife of a dignitary Sira had met, or a distant relative, or a friend of her mother's—but no, perhaps this was a goddess of whom Sira had not yet heard. . . .

The stone of the fountain was unblemished, practically new by all appearances, barely weathered—which struck Sira as strange: she realized she had never before seen freshly carved, new sculpture in the round. Apparently, it just wasn't being done anymore. She thought to ask her father why this was so, why the only other such sculptures she had seen, save for the occasional frieze on a government building or mausoleum, was weather-beaten, crumbling or partially destroyed, why it was that the beautiful fountains and statues were always old, deteriorating and historical—relics of the past—and how it could be so, when *this* could be done? The fountain was perfect and gorgeous and young and uplifting, as fresh and bright as the dawn after a rain-washed night.

Scattered about its lower rim were offerings of flowers and fruit, but there was no clue to the figure's identity, no identifying prop or symbol. The woman was dressed simply but elegantly in the classic tunica, stola and palla. An exposed swath of the tunica, from the shoulder to the waist, was so sheer and revealing that the woman may as well have been partially nude—the nipple of her right breast and her navel were clearly visible beneath the transparent stone fabric. Flanking the figure, on the steps below, were the figures of two young boys, one sitting, the other kneeling, each holding a tilted amphora from which water flowed and converged to cascade down the steps and into the pool below. The woman wasn't tall, yet she seemed to stand taller, and more comfortably so, than any sculpted figure Sira had ever seen. Her chin was lifted slightly, arms held loosely to her sides, hands relaxed. She was regal yet approachable, worldly wise yet light of spirit, nothing more and nothing less than a woman standing in the place where she stood, the whole of the earth as her kingdom and home. Sira found her enchantingly beautiful, shiningly intelligent, passionately feminine, faultlessly virtuous—all that a girl could want to see, all that a girl could want to be.

For Sira, it was turning out to be a most extraordinary and wondrous day, and in such a remote, nondescript town, no less. When her family had entered the town's gate, the place had promised nothing beyond the ordinary, and now she felt as if she were falling deeply in love for the second time within the hour, first with the boy, and now with this woman—

The boy . . .

She caught a glimpse of his curls disappearing into a street off of the far side of the square. She groaned, hesitated and, taking the white lily from her hair, laid it next to a blue lotus flower that someone had left next to the fountain's lower bowl. She looked up to the woman again, longing to spend at least a few moments more with her. She could have stood there forever. "Wait here," she said, and she ran to follow the boy, laughing as she realized she had just spoken aloud to a statue of stone and, moreover, had told it not to move.

ൠ

By the time she reached the entrance of the narrow street, the boy was no longer in sight. She plunged into the shadows, dodging a tottering widow in black and a scurrying feline in white. From the next intersection, she explored the alley to the left, to no avail, then followed a twisting flight of steps that led up and around to a gated dead end. Returning to the street below, she continued ahead, ducking beneath a line of drying laundry, turning down a lane which was narrower yet. Away from the town's center, the smoother paving stones gave way to knobby cobblestones, which gradually disappeared beneath a layer of craggy mud, dried since the last spring rain. She slowed to keep from twisting an ankle. The maze of walls and doors constricted, closing about her.

Attempting to circle back toward the square, she found herself in a squalid back alley of an older quarter. From open windows of dilapidated buildings, crude voices spoke the vulgar Latin rather than the predominant Greek—refugees from the besieged western provinces. Sira paused to catch her breath.

At the end of the alley stood what remained of the town's crumbling wall, with gaps in it large enough to ride a horde of Saracens through. But the day was too peaceful and perfect to be worrying about Saracens. Beyond the wall, a caravan was encamped on the rolling green foothills. The shadow of a cloud drifted across the painted wagons and brightly colored tents.

With a start, she leapt aside, just saving herself from being pulled into a darkened doorway by an old woman with rotting, flaking skin on her exposed limbs, reaching out with a clawed hand. The woman's faded purple stola clung precariously to her sagged, bony shoulders. Beneath the stola, the soiled tunica had nearly rotted away. Her fingernails were uncut, torn and yellowed. On her forehead was a festering reddish mark, in the shape of a cross, from the habitual tracing, before her every daily act, of the mark of her faith. Still grasping for Sira, she struggled to see through dimmed, clouded eyes.

"*Bella . . . bella . . .*" she muttered longingly, her voice cracked and broken.

Sira found a coin in her pouch and held it out.

As if burned, the woman yanked back her hand. She spit drily, bitterly at the ground.

Sira backed away, not understanding, her benevolence stung. She turned and made her way back toward the center of town, choosing a different route through the alleys and streets.

At an intersection from which she finally could see the square again, something caught her eye: on the keystone above an arched doorway was an engraving, a carved relief of a face—the face of the woman on the fountain, unmistakably so. Sira's heart jumped.

The door was half open. As she approached, she could see the boy inside, working in what at first appeared to her be a stonemason's shop. Heavy slabs, blocks, and columns of marble, granite, and limestone were arranged about the room and in the walled courtyard beyond. The stone was stacked, leaned and intermixed with intricately carved sarcophagi and statuary in various stages of finish and completion. The largest pieces were arranged along the walls and in the corners. Smaller figures and figurines, in myriad scale, were crowded along shelves that rose to the ceiling. The figures, all of the same masterful style and lifelike quality as those on the fountain, lent the shop the air of a village populated with strange and wondrous characters. Toward the shop's rear, an older, broad-backed man with rolling shoulders and a great sheaf of white hair stood at his workbench toiling over the details of a large frieze—from the marble, a platoon of soldiers in high relief struggled to emerge fully formed, to break free from the plane of their birth.

A fine white dust hung in the air, covering everything, including her young man, who sat astride a tall block of rough stone. The block was taller than Sira by half again, its mass positioned atop two iron bars laid in parallel on the floor. The boy was swinging a large hammer, driving iron wedges into a groove along the block's length.

Now it was she who was standing in the street, staring at him, watching him work—admiring the perfect coordination of his capable hands and calculating eyes, the athletic balance of his body, the strength of his legs binding him to the stone as he lashed at it rhythmically, exactly, unremittingly, as though taming a wild behemoth in the circus. The persistent ring of his hammer against the wedges dropped a half note in tone as a fracturing split opened down the side of the block. Without breaking rhythm, the boy coiled once more, twisting his torso and drawing the mallet back to full extension before unleashing a final, forceful blow that sent the wedge deep into the maw of the cleaving crack. The stone yawed open. The boy leapt to his feet. The sides of the block hit the ground with a boom that reverberated through the core of Sira's being.

When the cloud of dust parted, he was standing astride the cloven halves, his chest heaving, a foot on each block. He was looking straight at Sira, mallet in one hand, his other hand open and relaxed at his side, his body covered in white dust except for his eyes—eyes of hazel agate flecked with umber and gold, rimmed in moss green. He smiled.

Her knees nearly buckled beneath her. She turned and ran toward the square.

As she neared the fountain, she picked up speed, gathered her tunica, and without breaking stride, hurdled the rim of the lower bowl in a floating, weightless arc. Dashing and splashing, to the shock and displeasure of the locals nearby, she ran through the water spout of the young, happy elephant, jumping up as she passed beneath to pat the curve of its trunk. On the far side, she leapt onto the rim, turned and blew a kissed salute to her goddess above, first with one hand, then with the other, then with both—"Thank you! Thank you! *Thank you!*"

When she noticed the noise, heard the angry townspeople shouting and cursing her to Hades, she granted them a deep bow, dodged the whack of an elder's cane, and ran all the way back to the bazaar, where she had no answer at all to her mother's rebuke for her unexplained absence or to her father's question as to why she was wet to the bone—and perfectly happy to be so.

∽

She sighed. Today, the boy was still nowhere to be seen. She had been certain he would come again. It was well past the hour that he had appeared the day before. Had he lost interest in a mere trader girl passing through town? He probably already had a beautiful local girl under his spell, maybe two, maybe three. She retrieved a vial from her pouch and dabbed a touch of fragrance of jasmine at the hollow of her throat.

As she finished folding and stacking a column of handkerchiefs, her hopes of seeing him again were dimming. Diverting her thoughts, she sought out a prospect for her next sale. At the adjacent stall, a wealthy matron with expensive shoes and patrician posture was handling and sniffing the figs and cheeses, a well-dressed servant girl following dutifully behind and to the side. Sira maneuvered to the corner of her tent closest to the farmer's. "Your stola is quite lovely," she said. "It complements your skin color nicely."

The lady almost thanked her but cooled upon realizing that the girl addressing her with a queen's confidence was a plebeian at best. She turned again to her shopping. Thumbing an overly ripe fig, she cast a disapproving look at the farmer, who only shrugged in reply.

Sira warmed to the challenge. Her mother vacated through the rear flap of the tent to prepare the midday meal, having accepted, some time ago, that her daughter worked best alone. Sira raised herself to her full height, continuing to take the lady's measure.

"The fabric of your palla is from Sardis, yes?" she asked, casually, warmly, with elegant elocution. "You have excellent taste, ma'am."

"And you have a discerning eye for one so young," the lady replied, squeezing a last melon before shifting her attention to the belts hanging on the corner of Sira's tent. "You're younger than my daughters, and they can barely distinguish Egyptian linen from Tarentine wool."

"But surely you're too young to have children older than I. . . ."

The lady smiled, shaking her head, but she came further into Sira's tent to check through the basket of silver brooches, and in further yet to examine the bolts of richly dyed, patterned fabric.

"The indigo would go nicely with the pattern in your stola," Sira offered. "Your children must still be living at home, yes?"

"Only the youngest," the lady sighed, handing over a length of lightweight deep-orange wool for Sira to hold.

"This will be pretty to wear this summer." Sira turned it over in her hands. "It's good that you still have at least one of your children with you. Where are the others?" People's lives and stories never ceased to fascinate her.

While the lady enumerated those of her children who had gone out into the world, she indicated a length of yellow saffron-dyed linen, which Sira cut and folded while listening to answers to her questions about the lady's grandchildren. She arranged three embroidered handkerchiefs and a rolled band of tapestry atop the linen and wool while the lady reminisced on the bountiful markets of the Rome of her youth: before the barbarians came, everything had been better in Rome, the lady opined, while selecting an emerald green palla and a bolt of silk. Sira rolled the purchases into a bundle and tied them with bowed ribbon while commiserating as to the difficulty of finding well-made shoes these days for a decent price anywhere outside of Constantinople. The lady counted out what would have been a year's wage for the common laborer, as Sira handed the neat bundle to the servant, slipping the girl an extra handkerchief for herself. The lady insisted Sira come by her home later that afternoon to see her heirloom tapestries and her collection of jeweled ceremonial sandals. No excuse would be accepted.

As they glided off into the bazaar, the servant glanced back at Sira appreciatively. The pair passed the Phoenician and his saddles without giving them a second glance. The Phoenician's wife glared at Sira as if wanting to set Sira's hair on fire. Sira gave her a wink and a smile, and she closed her eyes to savor the wafting smells of the grilled lamb her mother was reheating.

"Which color do you think complements my skin tone better?"

It was the boy.

He was there, inside her tent, modeling a violet sash around his waist, a green sash draped over his shoulder. She kept her wits about her just enough to note that, in truth, the green went better with his curls. Suppressing a laugh, she felt the color rising to her cheeks.

He had made an attempt to clean himself up, but the stone dust was still lodged in the roots of his hair, beneath his fingernails and in the crevices of his ears. Though his tunic was thin and nearly worn through at the edges, he carried himself like a prince. She had a momentary thought of wanting to re-dress him in new things from her inventory, but with that imagery came complications she didn't know quite what to do with, raising her blush to a high crimson.

Her mother was still out of sight but not out of hearing.

"I'm sorry, sir," Sira replied in a lowered voice, "but may I suggest something more within your means?"

From a dusty box in the corner she selected a second-hand bronze spoon. Though it had been cleaned and polished, its handle was nicked, the bowl slightly dented.

Accepting it from her graciously, he allowed his fingers to brush hers for a moment longer than necessary. He examined the spoon approvingly, then leapt back, making several energetic thrusts and slashes with the utensil, as though at an invisible enemy.

"I was hoping you had something in steel, ma'am, but if you'll put an edge on this for me, it should serve well enough for those pathetic Persians I'll be meeting in the pass at Thermopylae this afternoon. And don't misjudge my means on account of my impoverished apparel—" he drew close enough to share a secret, dropping his voice to a whisper—"I often travel disguised as the mere apprentice of a sculptor to avoid having to deal with the attentions of all the young ladies who would wish to show their appreciation for my courage in defense of the empire."

She narrowed her eyes at him. "And *I* often travel disguised as the mere daughter of an itinerant trader to save from having to publicly chastise my insolent generals who like to parade through bazaars, attempting to impress the ladies with their likely stories. Besides, it's been nine centuries since Leonidas fought at Thermopylae—you're running rather late to die in that battle. However, it's your good fortune that we're having some trouble with the Huns again up north. You could do some good for what's left of the empire if you brought back a few of their heads. I may grant you an estate or two should you return victoriously— should you return at all."

They were chin to chin, his lowered, hers raised. As in her daydream, his lips were too close, his breath parting hers. And she was falling into his eyes.

"There is but one estate in which I am interested—" he said, quietly, letting his eyes wander down to her mouth. He dropped suddenly to a knee, lowering his head in deep genuflection—"my empress!"

A pair of dowdy matrons who had been thumbing through the fabric at the edge of the tent shook their heads disapprovingly and moved off just as Sira's mother emerged from the back. Noting the departure of the women and the bowing, dust-caked boy, she frowned darkly and indicated to Sira with an impatient flick of her finger that the boy was to be dismissed.

"Your food is ready, Sira. Hurry now before the other flies arrive to carry it off." She disappeared through the back flap.

Sira had noticed the boy shift slightly when her mother had used her name.

"*Get up!*" she hissed at him.

He didn't move.

"Get up, *please*," she implored. "You must go now."

He remained kneeling. "Your Highness would spare a modicum of dignity for her devoted and eternally loyal servant."

"If you insist. Rise then, General—?"

He looked up to her. "Myron. My name is Myron. And yours is *Sira. . . .*"

She wanted to run with him, run far away and to the top of his hill to live with him there forever.

"You should go now," she said.

He stood reluctantly but only to steal another long moment, gazing into her eyes. From behind the tent, her mother coughed loudly. Digging into the pouch on his belt, he found what was, by the lack of any jingling, the only coin therein. Pressing it into Sira's hand, he closed her fingers around it—

"For my sword," he said. He tucked the spoon into his pouch, patted it, and with a lingering glance, turned to go.

"Wait—" she called. She untied the blue silk sash from about her waist and held it out to him.

All of his playfulness fell away. There was a fearsome intensity to his gratitude as, with a tremble in his fingers, he took the sash into his hands, gently, as though to spare any harm to the pairs of embroidered birds in flight. Bringing the gift to his lips, he inhaled her fragrance, his eyes ablaze and dancing.

"My muse, I shall sculpt you a thousand times if I live long enough to do so."

He turned and strode out into the marketplace and down the street, her sash in his upraised hand, thrust to the sky. Sira watched it moving over the heads of the crowd like a blue sail across the sea, until it disappeared over the horizon.

She went to the rear of the tent to eat. She was ravenous.

Two

APOLLONIUS LAID HIS MALLET and chisel on the workbench. He bowed his head and closed his eyes as his hands began to move with a mother's care over the stone before him, his mind's eye following his touch, exploring the frieze he had been working on for nearly four months. His sight had deteriorated such that he was working almost as much by feel these days.

The irony was not lost on him that most of the commissions coming to him in his advanced age were for tomb décor. The piece was for yet another mausoleum facade; the scene, a military battle. He couldn't help but be pleased with the composition—the counterpoint and balance of the figures' poses and motion, the barely controlled violence achieved, the story well told. His horses were wild eyed, their nostrils flared, heads straining against the reins—panicked animals caught between holding to their masters' will and fleeing the tumult of battle. The thrusts of spears and swords, the anguish and devastation on the faces of the fallen, the desperate focus of those still on their feet fighting—one could almost smell the hot blood and the choking smoke in the air and hear the shouts of urgency, the cries of mortal pain, the clanging clash of denting metal. Through the chaos rode the imperturbable, fearless general ignoring the close danger of the flying arrows, commanding his troops to hold resolutely through the turn of the battle's tide.

With some minor refining and polishing here and there, the piece would be finished. With Myron's help, if they pushed through the afternoon and evening, it would be ready for delivery by morning. Apollonius let his hands come to rest on the bench. The work was good.

He ambled wearily through the rear door of the shop and into the grassless, walled plot behind—his quarry, he was fond of calling it, though over the years the yard had become more of a cemetery, with its crowded rows and stacks of stone blocks and slabs unused, cracked, or otherwise unfit. The midday sun was warm. His aching bones needed the heat. With a shiver, he shook the remaining chill out of his tunic. After another long winter in the north, it was hard not to think of balmy, beautiful Alexandria. But he wouldn't think of Alexandria, not today.

He hoped he had done the right thing in sending Myron back to the market, silk sash in hand. It was only yesterday that the boy had returned from the market with his token, but this was not the time for distractions or complications. Too much was at stake. Adult decisions had to be made. A great deal remained to be done today before they could leave on the morrow.

He eased himself into sitting on the monolith of stone that lay in the center of the yard. The rectangular block was half again as long as the sculptor was tall, its mass supported by a dozen wooden chocks which long ago had sunk into the ground beneath the stone's weight, weeds and wildflowers grown up around the edges. The city's dirt and soot and the yellow-green pollen of spring filled the chiseled crevices of its unfinished surface; only the smoother, rain-washed facets revealed a suggestion, here and there, of the luminescent whiteness within.

He sat for a time on the stone, unmoving, then bent forward, slowly, as far as he was able, until his beard hung between his knees, allowing the sun to soak through his tunic and into the pains that had taken up residence in his upper back and neck. The unrelieved tensions were the legacy of the repetitive, minute motions of honing and finishing, exacerbated by the strain of his weakening eyesight. The detail work was the most punishing. He was a large, densely muscled man, and despite his advanced age, he was strong enough still to swing his heaviest mallet from dawn till dusk—were there still the opportunity to do so. He would revel in the exercise of moving around a fresh, upright block of marble again, roughing out the large masses and shapes, committing the first acts, giving genesis to life rendered larger than life—*creatio ex materia* on the grand scale—if such work were still to be had. But maybe again, someday. Maybe again soon now. After the many long years of drought, the rainclouds of abundance were forming on the horizon. After years of wandering the desert, a land of milk and honey beckoned.

But first, there was much to be done—business to be concluded, accounts to be settled and closed, arrangements to be made—and all in a day's time. Hopefully Myron would return soon from his task, having resolved the matter of the sash, one way or the other.

With a wincing effort, the old sculptor lifted his legs and turned to recline along the stone's length for a few moments' rest.

CR

The marble block was one of two virtually identical pieces born on the isle of Paros. At the height of his professional success, those many years ago, Apollonius had journeyed to the famed quarries to select stone for a commission for the Alexandrian baths. He had been negotiating the order with the quarry-master when he noticed, off to the side of the workings, two of the most flawless, beautiful blocks of marble he had ever laid eyes on. Myth had it that Aphrodite had petitioned Poseidon to shake the earth beneath any town that erected a sculpture made of Parian marble, jealous as she was of the shimmeringly translucent skin of the figures sculpted thereof.

From his own savings, Apollonius had placed a deposit on the two pieces and, with the quarry-master's blessing, carved his name into a corner of each block, marking them as his own. It had taken him three years to pay for the pieces in full, and it was a joyful day when they were delivered to his workshop in Alexandria. But the blocks stood untouched for another year, then for two years more, and five more yet as he finished commission after commission. The money was good, the demand for his work high, and each purse bought a little more distance from memories of childhood hunger, destitution, and the forlorn helplessness in his mother's eyes. After many an exhausting day, he would sit in his workshop and gaze wistfully upon his Parian marbles, savoring the day when he would release the figures waiting within. They were to be his *magna opera*, the apogee of all of his knowledge and skill, the incarnation of his highest vision. To his clients' and friends' queries as to the subject matter, as to which gods or demigods were to be hewn from his precious marbles, Apollonius would only demur, allowing them to believe that he was as yet undecided, that he didn't yet know. But he knew. And the only person he had ever told was *her*. Which was only right, after their day together in Thebes. Especially after their day together in Thebes. Especially after the night that had followed the day . . .

But he wasn't going to think of Alexandria again, or of Thebes, or of the woman. Twenty years had passed, and he would live in the present—here, in the present, in this quiet, provincial town far north of Egypt. Here, lying atop the one block of Parian marble that remained.

The stone's warmth seeped into his bones. The sun glowed red through his eyelids. He let his body slip into peaceable quietude, the stillness broken only by the motion of his fingertips, which having found the marble through the dust, were making small, unconscious strokes and curves, caressing the virgin stone, eager and willing to begin the work, without their master if necessary, knowing by heart the music and wanting nothing more than to play, to carve away the irrelevant and let it fall to dust, to leave standing only the beautiful, the good, the important. A single strike of the mallet on the chisel would do it. A single act, and the beginning would begin. . . .

☙

His fingers were following rows of shallow grooves in a monolith of stone that wasn't smooth marble, but a hard, opaque quartzite that was pocked, cracked, and worn by long exposure to the elements. It was the base of a colossal seated figure, one of an identical pair of enthroned

Pharaohs, two solitary sentinels seated on the floodplain of the upper Nile, across the river from Thebes. The colossi were forty cubits tall, the height of twelve men, the distance between them equal to their height. The one before which he stood appeared to have been made from a single, massive block of stone.

For seventeen hundred years, the statues had guarded what remained of the Theban funerary temples and the necropoleis of the Egyptian kings. Day after day, the statues had been baked by the sun, strafed by sandstorms, flooded by the Nile; yet they remained standing, outlasting the Pharaonic dynasties, the conquering Assyrians, the Persians, the Greeks. The easterly statue had been damaged by an earthquake shortly after Cleopatra's death—the Romans had effected a repair with inferior sandstone—but the westerly of the two, the subject of Apollonius's present examination, was still whole, though ravaged by time and the elements. He speculated that the pair would likely outlast the rule of Constantinople as well.

He had taken a rare break from his work to join a commission of city leaders, intellectuals and artists who had made the long journey south from Alexandria and up the Nile to Thebes to study and inventory the ruins of the former capital. Though by nature and as a rule he avoided group activities, he hadn't been able to pass up the opportunity to see and examine for himself the famed Theban statuary. The group had already spent several days on the river's east bank, marveling at the ornately embellished pillars, pylons and gates of what remained of the temple complexes. The great Theban treasures touted in Homer's Illiad were long gone, of course, and several of the better-preserved temples had already been converted into Christian churches and monasteries, but the atmosphere of the sacred city was still indelibly impressed with the might of the dynastic rulers who had built it. The sheer scale and weightiness of the architecture and statuary would have exacted the intended effect on any normal man who might visit, be he domestic subject or foreign dignitary, leaving him to feel small and imminently crushable before the might of the Pharaoh.

At dawn that morning, the Alexandrians had ferried across the river to tour the necropolis of royal tombs built into the hillsides of the westerly valleys. Apollonius had slipped away to examine the pair of colossi firsthand. Though the morning was only hours old, the air on the desert's edge was already sweltering. He took a long drink from his goatskin bag.

He had been circling the base of the westerly sculpture, enjoying the silence, examining the hieroglyphs and smaller queenly figures carved on the front of the Pharaoh's throne, trying to determine what tools the artists could have used. The copper and bronze implements of their day would have been too soft and ineffectual for cutting stone as hard as quartzite. He was wondering if they had had access to emery, and if so, how they would have employed it, when, rounding a corner, he nearly bumped into her.

His focus had been at eye level. Her gaze had been upraised as she circled from the opposite direction, studying the statue's position relative to the path of the rising sun. Her surprised laugh was awkward and disarming, her smile bright against her sunburned cheeks and nose, wisps of brown hair sticking to her forehead and neck in the humidity. It was hardly the first time they had met, but it was their first time alone together. Brushing a strand of hair out of her eyes, she recovered her bearing.

"What is your opinion of it, Apollonius?" she asked, her tone professorial, the teacher querying the student. He had attended many of her classes and talks in Alexandria, though always in the company of the dozens of her students who had come from the four winds to attend her lectures on philosophy, mathematics and astronomy. She was along with the group to study the astronomical orientations of the Theban temples. As teacher, she was always the consummate professional, never breaking formal decorum; while patient and encouraging with her students, many of whom who were older than she, she rebuffed all attempts to breach the personal: in an age of men, she was, by necessity, as another man. Her intellect was dazzlingly quick, her knowledge of her subject matter wide-ranging and deep. Apart from her eyes, she was perhaps only on the prettier side of plain, but to Apollonius, her eyes revealed a mind that was a gorgeous force to behold, as agile and powerful as the honed body of an athlete in the Games, as graceful and lithe as any dancer on the amphitheatre stage. And she used that mind so well. He loved to watch her face as she calculated and measured, defined and proposed, considered and replied, countered and clarified—while delighting in all. In her presence, it was all he could do to keep from staring at her too rudely, and here, under the Theban sun, he realized he was simply staring at her again.

"What do you think of it, Apollonius?" she repeated.

He had been watching her wind-chapped lips. What little could be discerned of the feminine features beneath her somber scholar's cloak ever vexed his imagination. It was too hot in the desert for a cloak anyway.

He dragged his attention back to the statue. Its face had already crumbled away, but the original state of the figure and its twin across the way was easy enough to envision: a pair of stony, unmovable Pharaohs, like two fists pounded upon the desert floor, rendering unthinkable any challenge to their authority.

"I think the artist achieved his purpose, Teacher," he answered. "It would be the rare subject under this man's rule who could stand before these two and not be awestruck."

"Security was important to them, Apollonius, as it is to us now," she said. "The people have always some champion whom they set over them and nurse into greatness. . . . This and no other is the root from which a tyrant springs— when he first appears he is a protector." It was from Plato, whose philosophy she taught and followed.

Apollonius often lingered after her lectures as she took questions and offered explications on the finer points of the day's subject matter. He had been surprised to find himself participating when the topic touched on esthetics, and even more surprised to discover that his knowledge of art history and theory was deeper than that of the other students. In time, she began calling on him for his input on matters esthetic. In philosophy, however, he was among those in her class who favored Aristotle.

"*Men create gods after their own image,*" he offered, gazing up at the figure.

"Or is it Man who is the imperfect reflection?" She held the Platonic line. "Is imagery such as this statue Man's attempt to recognize and touch the Perfect? Surely the people who built these objects needed something to look up to, a vision of their ideal. In melding the man and the god, they deified their ruler."

"And in so doing, sealed the subjection of both their bodies and souls."

She searched her memory. "That's not from Aristotle. . . ."

"No . . ."

He was aware of her studying him as he continued studying the statue. Its style was static, unmoving, the figure more symbolic than human—a detached abstraction more form than content, an enthroned, omnipotent deity who wasn't to be known or understood or reasoned with by the common man, but simply to be recognized and obeyed. Apollonius didn't wish to start an argument, but he was thinking that Plato might have approved of these objects, if the pharaoh had been philosopher as well as king.

"You came to mind the other day, Apollonius," she said, breaking the silence.

"Oh?"

"I'm editing a work by a mathematician named Apollonius, on conics—on dividing a cone with a plane to make hyperbolas, parabolas and ellipses."

"Ah. I will look forward to reading it, Teacher."

"Yes . . ."

A northerly breeze was rising, pushing eddies of sand about their feet, dusting the crests of the small dunes. A sound between a whistle and moan rose as the wind carried the dust into a crack in the stone above, working its way through an ancient hollow to wear and hollow it further, atom by atom. On the day that the men had stopped working the stone, the elements had taken up the task, the wind following the rain, the rain following the sun. The daily work would not be through until the stone was reduced to dust upon the plain.

"I'm sure that you are aware," she said, "that some of the students, behind my back, have taken to referring to me as *Kheimon*, after the Goddess of Winter. I presume they disapprove of my demeanor."

He suppressed a smile. "I am aware of it, Teacher."

"I rather like the name," she said. "You are welcome to call me *Kheimon*."

"*Kheimon*. It is a beautiful name. I shall use it."

"Thank you, Apollonius."

They continued their respective contemplations in silence until the wind was such that they were shielding their eyes from the blowing sand and bracing their bodies against the stronger gusts. He thought she would have suggested by now that they leave, but she was still standing silently beside him, waiting, seemingly—for what, he did not know.

They needed to find shelter. He offered his hand to her. She declined it, but as he turned westward, toward the valley of the royal tombs, she turned and walked beside him.

છ

Once they entered the valley, they were sufficiently protected from the wind to converse again. They talked of all they had seen on the trip and of how different life must have been for teachers and artists under the Pharaonic dynasties compared to life in modern, cosmopolitan Alexandria, where conformity and dogma were practically sins, and reasoned, robust debate was still the rule. Alexandria had remained distinctly more Greek than Roman through the centuries of Rome's domination. With its great libraries, museum and schools, the city remained a center of culture, academics, science, medicine, and the arts. Despite the great physical damage wrought of late upon its secular institutions, it could still be ranked, arguably, as the most culturally advanced, liberal city in the world.

After following the valley's turn southward, they found themselves approaching the entrances of the tombs, cut into the sides of the cliffs. From one of the nearer openings emanated a murmur of voices and the unmistakable sing-song drone of their group's guide. With hardly a pause in their own conversation, the two walked on, passing the tomb's entrance without a second glance, neither suggesting an excuse for doing so.

It surprised and pleased Apollonius that she was willing to risk being seen alone with him. She was fastidious in regard to her reputation, and surely they both had been missed already—the rumors would begin as the hours wore on. In accordance with her ascetic Platonism, she strictly eschewed the physical pleasures as a matter of principle, her intellectual pursuits being, ostensibly, her sole passion. Rumor had it that she was completely celibate, though not all in Alexandria were convinced that her reputation wasn't cultivated of defensive necessity on her part. Nevertheless, she had remained above scandal or reproach—a woman of faultless virtue, according to the standards of most.

Farther up the valley, they approached a less obvious tomb entrance. Purchasing a torch from a blind man encamped in the portal's shade, they ventured inside.

By the lightly disturbed dust on the ground, the tomb was less trafficked than those down valley. The partially caved entrance opened into a larger vestibule, its walls

Part I: Genesis   IDOLATRY

and ceiling covered with foreboding imagery, painted and
carved, in warning to trespassers and grave robbers. A
passage of nearly a hundred steps led down into the tomb's
heart, and as they descended, the air became even hotter
and more stifling than it had been on the surface, further
exacerbated by the heat and smoke from the torch. When
they reached the lower level, the teacher removed her cloak
and, with neither comment nor apology, folded and placed
it neatly on the bottom step, leaving herself dressed in only
her light-weight cotton tunica, already damp and clinging
to her chest and slender hips. Apollonius provided no
outward indication of his approval.

While they explored the labyrinth of passages and
chambers, she deciphered the meanings of the murals and
hieroglyphs. In addition to her facility with the nuances of
the earlier language, yet another of her fields of expertise
was the culture's ancient custom and lore, evidently. Were
there no bounds to the depth and breadth of the woman's
knowledge? Apollonius was as excited by her mind as
by her body—perhaps even more so, he would have to
confess, if ever forced to confess.

Studying the carved reliefs himself, he noted the
similarities to an aspect of contemporary artistic style
he had first seen on a visit to Constantinople, a style
now dominant in the capital and increasingly prevalent
throughout the empire. The human figures in the Pharaoh's
tomb, like the colossi on the plain, seemed rendered as
symbols first and individuals second—when they were
identifiable as distinct individuals at all. Each figure was
more a game piece playing its pre-determined part, ranked
aesthetically and compositionally according to its role and

position relative to the other pieces, each according to its place, role and rank in the societal system.

He was holding the torch, circling a pillar, studying the figures carved in relief, when he realized he was causing the pillar's shadow to move across a wall mural that his companion was studying. He grimaced. "My apologies for the eclipse, Kheimon. The moon shall not come between us again."

"Thank you, Apollo. You are forgiven."

"I could play Plato and make a shadow of a bounding hare on the wall for you."

In her wry smile he thought he caught a momentary glimpse of what she might have been as a young girl.

"Or you could go back to addressing me as 'Teacher,'" she said, chastising.

He was enjoying her company immensely. He returned to studying the art.

It had taken a thousand years of halting, step-by-step progress from what the Egyptians had created here in the tombs to the heights of artistic mastery achieved by the Greeks. The Greeks' glory had reigned a mere four hundred years, followed by four hundred years of the Romans copying and emulating the Greeks. Since the founding of Constantinople, the standard had been sliding in the reverse direction: presently, there was a clear trend toward making artistic figures less human and more symbolic again. Moreover, what human qualities the figures were granted were becoming distorted, even grotesquely so: human heads were now being rendered well out of proportion to their bodies, and the bodies were squat, blocky, amorphous, detached from their surroundings in a seemingly intentional attempt to undo and reverse, as quickly as possible, what so many earlier generations had struggled to achieve. The Greeks had succeeded in developing the techniques necessary to accent, highlight and celebrate a man's every admirable and beautiful quality—spiritual, intellectual and physical—while the current crop of craftsmen apparently saw nothing lovely or laudatory in the individual man at all, and visually brutalized him for it. By the evidence the present-day artists were now providing, a man's only possible significance to his contemporaries, the only aspect of his person worthy of portrayal, was his pious devotion to his deity and his status within the religious and social hierarchy.

To the best of Apollonius's knowledge, there were less than a handful of artists still working in the traditional style. He was unaware of anyone still teaching the classic standards, ideals and techniques. His own teacher, in southern Greece, had taught only three students, who had fled upon their teacher's death during the Goths' sack of their town. The friends survived the year-long odyssey to Egypt, on foot, unable to afford ship's fare, only to have the most talented killed by the authorities for sculpting a pagan god for an underground temple. His remaining friend had quit sculpting altogether, had married, started a family, and toiled at simple masonry work for years before dying of exhaustion or depression, or both. Apollonius had set up shop in Alexandria, where with hard work, perseverance and skill, eventually he thrived. Occasional interaction with the blacksmith, maker of the best tools and hardware Apollonius had ever seen, was the extent of his social life. When the two spoke, it was with mutual respect and admiration.

Now here, in the remote Theban desert, he was profoundly grateful for the companionship of the extraordinary woman who had accompanied him, alone, into the depths of an ancient tomb, though he was still unsure as to why or how she had come to be with him.

They arrived at the doorway to the final chamber. The room was smaller and, if possible, even more claustrophobic than those preceding. Within, carved from a block of fine red sandstone, lay the sarcophagus. Somewhere in Thebes or on the western floodplain would have been an enormous mortuary temple built for the cult worship of this god-king during and after his lifetime; the planning of his temple and tomb would have started on the very day of his ascension to the throne. And here, in this very room, was the final goal, the purpose of an entire generation's aspirations and labors: the proper positioning of their Pharaoh in death, so that he would be able to rise to the heavens thereafter.

Both explorers were soaked in perspiration. Apollonius had been following a half-step behind her, allowing the occasional glimpse by torchlight of the curves and hollows of her profile beneath the clinging tunica. She had stopped in the doorway. Coming up beside her, he watched a bead of perspiration trace down her neck and over her clavicle to disappear in the vale between her breasts, her chest rising and falling with quickened breath, her nipples standing against the transparent, wet cotton, her eyes afire with curiosity. In the presence of death, she seemed more alive than ever.

They approached the sarcophagus in silence. The walls of the room, here at the end of the Pharaoh's story, were more soberly and austerely adorned, as if there were little left to be said when it came to the fact of death itself.

The thick slab of stone atop the sarcophagus was slightly ajar. With all his strength, Apollonius was able to push and slide the lid just far enough for it to be seen that the final resting place was—empty.

The absence of the body seemed to upset the scholar deeply, breaking the paradigm of the world in which she had become immersed, disrupting the order of expectation. She was too rational, too much the scientist, to give any credence to the notion of a man actually having risen from the dead and ascended. A mere grave robber had undercut an entire culture's immense efforts, the life's work of a generation of men, rendering their dreams and hopes and endeavors not only meaningless, but transparently so. With the body gone, the whole of the tomb, indeed the whole of Thebes, seemed empty.

"This was not how it was supposed to be. . . ." she said.

With the smoke from the torch swirling about them, the air was sweltering and thin, suffocating. Her body began to sway. He reached out to steady her. The weight of the entire hill above seemed pressing in and down on them.

They retraced their steps in silence. At the bottom of the stairs, she insisted on putting her cloak back on. Reluctantly, he assisted. Each ascending step brought them closer to light and life. When they regained the surface and emerged, Apollonius squinted, stretched his chest and took a deep draught of fresh air, grateful to have managed on his own what no dead pharaoh had ever accomplished with the assistance of a kingdom of enslaved men. And he had done it with a living, breathing queen by his side, no less.

CR

The blind man led them to a nearby water cache, where they drank deeply and refilled the goatskin. Following his directions, they found the path that wound up and out of the top end of the valley, leading to a pyramid-shaped peak dominating the skyline. It was an arduous hike in the heat, with the final leg approaching and following the uppermost ridge, but on the summit they were rewarded with a cooling northerly breeze and sweeping views. Far below, their fellow travelers could be seen making their way back toward the mouth of the valley. To the east were the colossi on the plain and the winding umbilical of the Nile. Across the shore lay the ruins of Thebes and the hazy blue horizon of hills beyond.

They sat and rested, their conversation turning to things beyond ancient Thebes—the current cultural trends, the latest scientific and medical discoveries, the labyrinthine politics of Alexandria. The hours slipped away as they discussed the intricacies of the age-old feuds between the Alexandrian Egyptians, Jews, Christians, and Pagans, the tensions which at regular, almost predictable intervals would erupt into deadly rioting. In her philosophy class, she often found it challenging to keep the peace between the students. Even with her facility with Platonism, by which she endeavored to build bridges, to highlight the commonalities between the competing ideologies, the veneer of civility could break down with alarming speed when the students could claim equal validity for their religions' respective divine inspirations. While working to find a solution to the validity problem, she had become adept at steering their attentions to less divisive issues.

The setting sun painted the sky in shades of velvety peach, rendering to hues of plum and pomegranate. Venus and Mars appeared above the horizon, and as the stars came out, one by one, the sculptor and teacher laid back to watch the night sky unfold until it was a blanket of shimmering light so thick that the smallest hole couldn't be found in it. He obliged her to identify the stars and constellations. She named more than he could have possibly recalled afterwards. She related a theory she was developing and her evidence for it, that the Theban temple complexes may have been laid out in a configuration reflecting the constellation Aries above. It sounded entirely plausible to Apollonius.

The subject of astronomy led to ruminations on the mythic stories of how the constellations were named, and talk of myths turned to discussion of drama, which led to musings on poetry and recitations of their respective favorites. Watching for falling stars, they contemplated religion and metaphysics and the nature of Man.

Though the day's heat had gone, the evening remained warm, the universe turning slowly above. It was long after midnight, during a comfortable silence fallen between them, when it occurred to him that he was lying next to one of the most renowned intellectuals of the civilized world, the unbreakable enigma herself, the untouchable one. Untouchable, yet here she was, the goddess of winter, lying alone in the desert next to *him*, Apollonius the sculptor, as though they had been close friends for years. He was trying not to ask himself why.

"*No one loves the man whom he fears,*" she said, breaking the silence, quoting Aristotle.

No one loves the man whom he fears. Surely she wasn't thinking again of the Pharaohs. He pondered it a while before choosing his next words carefully.

"You do not fear me, Kheimon?"

"I do not."

It was a sacred silence beneath the stars, with everything in its right and proper place, two of the shimmering orbs above so close together that their lights appeared to be fusing, as though that they could not be kept apart. He could feel the tangible reality of her body close to his own. He could feel the space between them breaking.

A star streaked across the sky. As casually as he was able, he sat up. She did so in turn, crossing her arms around her knees, holding her gaze on the stars. Silhouetted in soft blue, she was the loveliest thing he had ever seen.

A breath of coolness rose from the valley. She shivered and hugged her knees close. He moved over and behind her. Parting his legs, he shifted forward, folded his arms around her, and held her gently.

She didn't respond. Her body remained rigid and still. She said nothing.

They stayed that way, watching the heavens above, with ancient Thebes below and the moonlight reflecting white on the black ribbon of the Nile. It wasn't until the stars to the east began surrendering to rising bands of indigo and pink that he felt her recline slightly, allowing her shoulders, but only her shoulders, to rest against his chest. When the first of the sun's rays pierced the horizon, her body shook, then shook again. Tears flowed down her cheeks as she broke, releasing. Leaning back, she melted into his warmth and strength.

He held her close and let her cry.

Three

THE SUN WAS CLIMBING above the desert horizon. A kestrel lifted on a warming current of air, circling below the peak on its first hunt of the day.

"We should go," she said.

Her eyes had dried. Their group's boat was due to depart northward for home later that morning.

Avoiding the long return through the valley, they followed a more direct, steeper path down to the floodplain. She took his hand as he offered it over the more difficult passages. When they reached the plain, she was still holding it. They passed several herders along the road who smilingly greeted the couple. She seemed comfortable enough, but when they came within sight of the ferryman, she let go of his hand and shifted a pace aside. They crossed the river in silence; he, sitting on a coil of rope; she, standing apart.

Upon debarking in Thebes, she hesitated, as if wanting to say something, but she turned and walked away without a word or backward glance.

It wasn't until days later, as they were sailing with the group downstream and homeward, that he finally found her alone again, standing near the prow. To his knowledge, no one had said anything about their absence that day or about the possibility of their having spent the night together. If anyone had noticed, they didn't seem to care. He struck up a casual conversation with her. She was friendly and sociable enough, yet professionally distant again.

He was a patient man. He did not press.

Back in Alexandria, she went on with her teaching and he with his sculpting. He attended her classes, staying afterwards for the discussions, as before, but she was always in the company of at least two or three other students, even as she departed for home. One day in the early spring, he was surprised and delighted when she asked if she could bring a group of students to his workshop.

On the day of the visit, she was wearing a blue lotus flower in her hair, its stem tucked into one of her pinned-back braids. It was the first time he had seen her permit even the smallest feminine touch to her outer appearance. He thought she looked stunning.

After giving the students an introduction to the tools, materials and techniques of his trade, he presented a brief history of the treatment of the human figure, covering what he knew of the figurative arts from the ancient Egyptians through to the Assyrians, to the Mycenaeans, the Persians, the Etruscans, the Phoenicians, through the stages of Greek development and mastery, through the Roman copying of the Greeks, through the plundering by the emperors of Constantinople to the present state of the declining, disappearing art. To demonstrate the evolution of sculpture over the ages, he drew from his collection of artifacts, much of which he had salvaged himself from ruins explored while traveling. The students particularly taken with the pieces and parts of elegant limbs and digits he had found on a construction site in Athens.

He was encouraging them to pass the pieces around, to experience firsthand the seductive, smooth texture of the marble skin, the sensuous elegance of the rendered forms, when he noticed she had detached from the group. She was standing in front of his workbench, looking up at a bronze figurine, a male nude no taller than the length of a man's forearm. It stood alone on a shelf above the bench, in a clearing between an assortment of tools. While the students compared the Athenian artifacts, Apollonius went to stand beside her.

"Did you make this one, Apollonius?" she asked.

"No, Kheimon."

"May I ask where it came from?"

"It belonged to my master, my sculpture teacher. It was given to him by his teacher, who found it when digging through what he believed to be the ruins of one of the workshops of Phidias."

"*The* Phidias?" She was not easily impressed. "The Phidias who sculpted—?"

"Yes. My teacher's teacher was convinced that this piece was a modello—a study for a much larger, monumental work to be created. It may have been crafted by a fellow artist or by one of Phidias's students, but it was found with several other modelli for Phidias's colossal works—the *Athena Parthenos* and the Olympian *Zeus*, among others."

"But the enlargement of this one was never built?"

"Not that we know of."

"Is it god or man?"

He smiled wistfully. "It was from a time when it was becoming difficult to tell the difference, yes?"

"But there is no evidence as to its identity?"

"It is a man, is it not?"

"A man with god-like qualities—the noble visage, the air of authority, how he stands just so—a man, or perhaps a god who had yet to become known, had yet to introduce himself."

"And yet, it is a man."

"There was an altar in Athens dedicated to *Agnostos Theos*—'the unknown god.'"

He considered it. "Perhaps the Greeks were onto something with that," he said, "if even by accident."

"Many inventions and discoveries have been born of accidents and midwived by nurturing minds," she said, musing. "But this figurine—it was born in Athens' great age, then lost and buried, resurrected by a sculptor who handed it down to his student, who in turn became your teacher, and your teacher gave it to you—"

"Not quite. My teacher was murdered in the street by Alaric's Goths, when they plundered our town on their march to Athens. I took the sculpture from the workshop as my friends and I were escaping. It was the one thing I was able to carry away from Greece. We walked."

"It isn't light, I presume."

"Rather heavy for its size."

"It was the most important thing. . . ."

"Yes . . ."

"Other than yourself, of course."

He chose to take it as a compliment—

"Thank you, Kheimon."

"And you are planning to sculpt the enlarged version yourself."

She had stated it as fact. Would her perspicacity never cease to surprise?

"Someday, hopefully," he answered. "But this figure seems more a sketch to me, an idea. I don't think that its essence had yet been fully worked out. There is something of an incompleteness about it, as though, if the figure were alive, it might have been mere moments away from declaring its theme, its identity—but as presented here, it seems yet on the verge, not quite ready. I can sculpt neither uncertainty nor uncertainly. I must know what it is that I am creating."

"Man is a being in search of meaning." She had quoted Plato again.

"I've always wondered," he said, "if perhaps that is why Phidias hadn't followed through with the project—because he wasn't yet certain of its meaning. Maybe he was trying to work it out, but had been able to come only so far, to approach it only this closely. He had sculpted the gods magnificently and with great confidence, but this, I think, was something new. Other cultures had their gods, of course, but the Greeks, their gods were becoming more and more human—"

"—or less inhuman . . ."

"This figure seems to me to be more of an embodiment of a question, a question to which they were trying to find the answer."

"The philosophers were pursuing the answer," she said. "They weren't content with mere superstition. They were trying to find the meaning of it all, of how the universe works, studying and dissecting the world around them, seeking to determine Man's place in it. Pythagoras was measuring. Socrates, asking. Plato, deducing. Aristotle, inducing. . . ."

It was as if they were back in Thebes again together, lying on the summit of the hill, gazing up at the night sky.

She studied the sculpture, musing. "It is still the most important thing, you know."

"Yes, the most important thing . . ."

Looking at her, at the way she looked up at the modello, reverently, with clear eyes and purity of curiosity, with her hunger for truth, it was hard to imagine anything more important.

"Maybe the sculpture wasn't the question," he ventured, "but an attempt at the answer."

"Maybe the answer is right here in front of us, Apollonius. Maybe it is right here with us."

"Perhaps you will identify it for me, Philosopher. I hope so, as I would like to get on with sculpting it."

"Perhaps you will show it to me, Artist, as I would like to get on with identifying it."

She was looking at the modello, but smiling with him. They dueled well together, danced well, each the better for it.

"Will it be in bronze then," she asked, "your grand enlargement?"

"Bronze would never be allowed these days. Bronze is too closely associated with all things pagan and idolatrous. You were here when the Christians destroyed the temples, yes?"

"I was twenty-one. . . ." She shuddered, trying to keep the memories down. She failed. There were the screams again of her dying friend, whose abdomen had been cut through. There was her father, the great mathematician, stumbling home, his face brutalized, his leg broken, the mob's response to his reasoned protests against the destruction. There was the body of the young man she loved, crushed beneath the fallen statue he had been trying to save, having finished sculpting it only days before. It had all been destroyed, the stone broken, what remained of the museum and library burned, the metal melted, the bodies left where they lay. But she was stronger now. Much stronger, and wiser. She had learned, with Plato's help, to detach, to float above, to find solace in transcendence, that everything below was mere shifting shadows and imperfect reflections—and who could be hurt by shifting shadows and reflections? Philosophy was always there to save her, to take her away, despite the occasional temptation to let herself fall back again into the carnal earthiness of the material, to live simply and fully in the physical world that the people on the street seemed to take for granted, to allow her soul and body to be caught up in its pleasures, to be enveloped and swept away by . . .

The powerful, raw physicality of the man standing next to her was intoxicating. She closed her eyes against it for a brief moment—and rose above.

"The Apostle Paul," she continued evenly, "when he visited Athens, claimed that the Greek's unknown god was the Christian deity, whom the pagans had yet to recognize as the one true god."

"That Paul was a clever opportunist and a sharp marketer," Apollonius retorted. As he said it, he noticed the eyes of one of the students, a pale, chinless fellow in an undyed monk's robe, locking onto him.

"Mind that one," the teacher said, in a quiet aside. "That's Peter, one of Cyril's deacons."

"Cyril? Cyril the new bishop? Let me show you something." He directed her attention to his current work in progress, propped on the workbench. It was a large carved relief for the residence of a wealthy patron, featuring a pair of lounging lovers in a pastoral scene, with satyrs and cupids playing on the periphery. He pointed to a glowering imp, peering out from behind a bush.

She suppressed a smile. "It's a true likeness, Apollonius. But don't underestimate Cyril. He has eyes and ears everywhere. His ambition is boundless."

"As is my disdain for pompous tyrants in the making." He turned his attention again to the modello. "No, the Christians wouldn't abide a statue in bronze. Bronze would be ideal, but stone might be acceptable, stone being more generically Roman, yes? And if the enlargement weren't on such a colossal scale or exhibited in a public place, but perhaps in a private residence . . ." He glanced at his two blocks of Parian marble, standing together in the corner.

"It would be lovely in marble," she said. "But those appear to be a set. What would you do with the other?"

"The other? The other is easy. I've already decided upon the other. The figure is already pictured perfectly in my mind's eye." He was looking at her unapologetically, directly. "They would make the perfect pair, I think. . . ."

It took her a moment, but with a sharp inhalation, she turned and stared at him with a penetrating intensity. "Perhaps I should fear you," she said quietly, her eyes flitting between his.

"Or perhaps the sun will rise again," he answered, hoping he hadn't lost her, hoping he hadn't revealed too much.

The students, growing impatient, were shifting about, watching uncomfortably. One of them began tapping the fingers of a broken marble hand on the table. Apollonius turned. He had forgotten about them.

He concluded his presentation by showing and explaining his work in progress, choosing not to mention the likeness of the bishop. The deacon Peter noticed, regardless.

"Who is that?" he asked, pointing with eager suspicion at the impish figure.

"No one important." Apollonius answered, distracted.

"Really? I do believe I recognize him."

"If you must know then, there is an old myth about a priest who, having convinced himself that he would use great power for great good, wished to be Pharaoh, and he wanted it so fervently that he would employ any means necessary to achieve his end. One day, he was preparing a dagger with a deadly poison for use against anyone who might stand in his way, but he momentarily forgot where he laid it. Accidentally sitting upon it, he soon died a painful death. The gods saw fit to reincarnate him as the misbegotten spawn of a careless peasant girl and a libidinous donkey, as a reminder to all who crossed paths with him that it is wise to watch one's behind around aspiring asses. Other than that, he's not important."

A young Jewish scholar coughed loudly to cover his laugh. Others in the group didn't try as hard to hide their amusement. The deacon attempted to protest but had been rendered speechless. The only person in the room whose opinion Apollonius cared about lodged a look of concerned disapproval, but he could only be pleased that she cared.

As the group was leaving, he drew her aside.

"When may I see you again, Kheimon?" he asked.

"In class tomorrow, of course—" she had already cooled again—"if you are planning to attend."

It wasn't the response he had been hoping for.

As she was turning to go, she softened and said, "You know, the modello does remind me of someone."

"Yes?"

She almost answered.

"Apollonius, please be careful of offending those in power. Many of the Christians, perhaps most, are fine and good people, and I believe that there can be peace, that they are capable of seeing that their philosophy and that of the Jews and of Plato share more in common than not, but you weren't here when—"

"Alaric and his Goths were Christian too, you know."

"Yes. I had forgotten. I'm sorry. . . . I will see you in class tomorrow then?"

"Tomorrow, and tomorrow . . ."

Again, she turned to leave.

"I think Plato was wrong," he said.

She spun around, brows knitting.

He had decided to take one more chance. "If Plato had ever met someone as brilliant and beautiful as you, he could never have confused a mere shadow with the divine being who cast it."

She took the blue lotus from her hair and placed it in his hand. Her eyes were wet as she turned and walked out the door, into the sunlit day, her shadow following.

It was the last time he ever saw her.

Four

FIRST CAME A LOW, DISTANT RUMBLING, then a rise in the pitch of voices far away, an urgency in the barking of the dogs, the silence of the birds—sensations on the periphery, felt before heard.

There was panic somewhere.

My tools. I need my tools. I cannot leave without my tools.

Then came the sudden realization that she might be in danger too, that he should find her and quickly—but his block of marble had been carved into a deep sarcophagus and he was lying in the bottom of it, looking up at the blue rectangle above. Try as he might, he couldn't move his arms or his legs. All he could do, as the darkening smoke wafted across the sky, was call out for her—

Kheimon, Kheimon, Kheimon . . .

He woke with a start, in a palpitating sweat, squinting up at the sun. He was still lying atop the marble in his yard, five hundred miles north of Egypt.

It had been years since he had last had the dreams. He listened carefully, but the world seemed quiet enough, at peace. The noises of the midday town seemed the normal ones. Normal was good.

He closed his eyes again.

The last he had seen of Alexandria was twenty years ago from the stern of a ship, with nothing in his possession but his bag of tools, a small purse of money and, wrapped in his cloak, the bronze figurine.

Before leaving, he had made just enough time to send a quick note to the blacksmith, revealing where the rest of his money was cached, with a request that it be used to ship his Parian marbles to an address to be forwarded later, if the blocks hadn't already been destroyed or stolen. The marble had followed him months later, arriving together with a leather-wrapped package from the blacksmith containing a set of beautiful new chisels and a new mallet, the initial "A" inlaid in ivory in its polished acacia handle. The craftsmanship was, of course, superb. The tools were accompanied by a note:

> For the last of the fine masters, my finest steel.
> You are missed, my friend. I am reduced to making
> sharp tools for dull men.—Hephaestius

The last of the fine masters. It had seemed so even to Apollonius himself, though it no longer mattered.

The town he had moved to was everything Alexandria was not—quiet, mundane, obscure, far from the seats of power, yet far enough from the borders to be relatively secure. But the peace came at a price: there were few residents in the town wealthy enough to afford fine art or high craft. After securing a space suitable for a workshop, he walked door to door to the wealthier homes, introducing himself and his work. No one in town had ever heard of him—no one would let him so much as cross their threshold. It took him all of two days to exhaust the options available within the town walls. He packed his tools and walked out into the countryside to call upon the rural estates, circling back into town every few weeks to check for any messages.

The first job secured was for restoration of an older villa—cleaning the friezes on the facades, repairing the capitals of the columns. At another villa, he cleaned and restored several mosaics. He had never worked on a mosaic before, but having labored for many years next to the mosaic artists in Alexandria, he had learned enough to get by. Out of necessity, he took several jobs of straight masonry work. But his reputation in the region gradually grew for producing excellent artistic carving and for reliably delivering jobs on time and on budget. The commissions began to trickle in from surrounding towns, then from cities farther away. After several years, he was doing as much work in the shop as out.

His blocks of Parian marble lay untouched in the back yard, side by side.

With the distraction of work, life was tolerable enough during the days, but the blackness of the nights was unrelenting. Even worse than the nightmares was the simmering torment of anger, bitterness, and despair that had taken root in his soul and was spreading like a tumor, creeping inexorably out of the night and into the day, into his work, infecting his scenes with worrisome frequency. Faces on his friezes contorted in rage, figures twisted in pain, pushing out from the stone, and he couldn't find his way free of them. During the times when the anger had exhausted itself into remission, he would find himself carving figures of such abject loneliness that looking at them in the evenings was enough to make him weep.

It was just so, late one evening. He had worked through the night and day prior on another mausoleum frieze, trying to reach a state of exhaustion and numbness that would overwhelm him enough that he could sleep. In the scene, the mourners surrounding the dead body were distraught; all were focused on the deceased except one figure—a man who had turned to look out at the viewer, searching for an unfindable answer. His face was sorrow incarnate.

Apollonius sat on the floor, his head fallen, his body bowed over and so tired that he could no longer lift his arms, and still his soul hurt too much to rest. The tears began to fall, making silent splashes in the marble dust on the floor, as the night's last candle burned low.

He sniffed—and heard an echoing sniff, disembodied, not his own. He sniffed again. Another small sniffle answered. He opened his eyes to find a toddler sitting on the floor next to him, gazing up at the funereal scene, tears rolling down the urchin's dust-caked cheeks. He was begrimed but beautiful, with auburn-bronze curls and hazel eyes flecked with umber and gold. The bedraggled cloth draping his little body was a dirty rectangle of coarse, undyed wool, a hole cut out for the head. Of the pins meant to hold the sides of the cloth together, one had torn loose, the other had ripped nearly away and was hanging by only a few threads.

Seeing Apollonius's distraught face, the boy began crying all the harder. The two looked at each other and cried on, emptying the depths of their grief until Apollonius could no longer bear the pathos, such a pitiable outpouring from such a flawless creature who surely could know so little yet of pain, a mere child with the prospect of a lifetime of joys before him. The scene had become an absurd injustice, and from somewhere in Apollonius's soul, from a place he had thought had long died, something rose through the thick sadness, bubbling upwards to escape—

He laughed.

It was an agonized laugh, a pained laugh, but a laugh nonetheless, and the boy, in turn, laughed at the sound of it. Apollonius put his arm around the boy and pulled him close. The two cried and laughed together until the candle flickered its last, until the forlorn faces on the frieze had vanished into the blanketing darkness, until sleep overcame the night.

ଓ

At dawn, he awoke on the cold floor to find the boy curled in his arms, the disheveled bronze curls matted about the tear-streaked face, long lashes resting on cherubic cheeks.

Gently, carefully, he picked the boy up and carried him to the work bench, where he tucked a piece of marble under his head and covered him with his own cloak. As quietly as he could manage, he arranged twice the usual quantity of wood on the fire and stoked the embers into a warming blaze. Finding nothing noiseless to do in a sculptor's workshop, he sat down in the back doorway to take in the morning sun and read a little from his copy of Sophocles, a pleasure he hadn't enjoyed in years.

The boy awoke an hour later to greedily devour a small pyramid of figs and a half-round of bread placed before him. To Apollonius's questions about his home and parents, he would only shake his head and continue eating. When asked his name, he wouldn't tell it, or didn't know it, or didn't have one.

Later that morning, Apollonius picked up the child and carried him around the neighborhood, certain that his panicked parents would be combing the streets for him. But no one knew or recognized the little fellow. Over the next week, he scoured the town, becoming increasingly concerned—not only did no one seem to recognize the boy, no one would take him in either. There had been a drought the summer before, and food was scarce. The monastery was already overflowing with unhappy orphans. Some of the poorer families were selling their children to dealers, who in turn were selling them into servitude to the wealthy in the larger cities. The baker speculated that the child may have been with a caravan that had passed through town several weeks prior, but no one expressed any interest in the boy, no more than they might in a stray kid goat.

The weeks wore on. Whenever the child looked upon the sad faces on the mausoleum frieze, he would start crying again. Apollonius began covering the piece with canvas when he wasn't working on it. He set about carving a few freestanding animals out of wood for the child to play with. A small menagerie was brought into existence, followed by a phalanx of soldiers and a contingent of cavalry. Noting the boy's enthusiasm with the military figures, Apollonius constructed a toddler-sized chariot out of cedar, complete with an axle and working wheels, and an extra wheel on the front so that Apollonius could pull it along with a length of rope. The boy would stand in the chariot when they went to market, nodding and waving to the passersby like a young Alexander returning victorious from his conquests, his bronze curls bouncing and blowing in the breeze. Apollonius fashioned a little laurel wreath for the boy's head and named him Myron, after the great Athenian sculptor of old.

Inevitably, the stray child attracted a stray dog, to the dismay and firm resistance of the master of the house. The cur was a big, gentle brute, a mongrel of a mountain dog with curls matching Myron's own in color. The dog would be named Hammurabi. In retaliation for having been conquered, Apollonius designed a harness for the dog and trained it to pull the chariot. The three made a fine picture about town. It wasn't long before Myron was old enough to ride the chariot to market on his own. The merchants would fill his shopping list, and Myron would walk beside the loaded chariot as Hammurabi pulled it home, as proudly as the finest steed in the emperor's parade.

In the shop, Myron learned to sweep, dust and clean. He took their clothes to the washerwomen at the river, delivered messages around town, tended the fire and learned to cook. But his favorite thing was to watch Apollonius work. With rapt attentiveness, for hours on end when allowed to do so, he would sit and study whatever Apollonius was doing, asking only the occasional question. As the seasons passed, Apollonius taught him to use the rasp, the file, and the emery, to do some of the lighter finishing and polishing, which the boy learned to do exceptionally well and with great care. Myron would plead to be allowed to use the chisels, but Apollonius would permit him only the nicked, duller tools with which to practice, and these were to be used only on scrap stone or wood in the yard. It would be years yet before the boy might be allowed to use the good chisels on the good marble—the good tools were too expensive to risk being ruined, and expensive stone could too easily be damaged. On the works in progress, a single chisel strike made in error could do irreparable harm to weeks or months of work. Myron was allowed to practice on the scrap stone in the yard, making straight edges and grooves and basic shapes such as spheres, cylinders, domes and pyramids. He picked up Apollonius's habit of patting the blocks of Parian marble whenever passing them.

The earth had circled the sun, according to the theory of Aristarchus, perhaps seven times since the boy came into the sculptor's life, when upon returning home from an errand one afternoon, Apollonius found, sitting in the back doorway, quietly and still, a white rabbit. The rabbit was staring at him, one ear up, the other laid over. Hammurabi lay in the corner on his pallet, glancing uneasily from the rabbit to Apollonius and back.

Apollonius was disappointed in the caliber of dog they had adopted. He made a shushing wave at the rabbit to frighten it off—but the animal didn't move. Hammurabi whined and laid his head on his paws.

On closer inspection, the rabbit was found to be carved of limestone, its pink nose delicately painted as were its brown eyes. It was an impressive piece of work—most likely an antique, restored and repainted, originally from somewhere in the Cyclades, was Apollonius's best guess. Whoever owned it was going to be upset to find it missing.

"Myron!" he called.

Myron appeared from the back yard, an unconvincing expression of surprise and questioning on his face.

"Myron, where did you get this?"

"I got it from nowhere, Master," the boy said chirpily.

"Did you take it from someone's villa?"

The boy shook his head.

"Did it come from someone's shop? This is an expensive piece, Myron. It must be returned immediately."

"I took it from nowhere, Master."

"It must be returned to where it came from, Myron."

"It cannot be returned, Master."

Apollonius was losing patience. "Punishment for thievery is a public lashing and restitution to the owner of at least twice the value. Moreover, our reputation and honor are at risk, and I won't abide any damage to our good name."

"It appears to be a real rabbit, Master. Perhaps Hammurabi brought it in from the fields. It looks as if it is too scared to move."

Now the boy was just being impertinent—fearless, but impertinent—which Apollonius found entirely disarming yet entirely unacceptable. He sent Myron to bed without dinner.

The next morning, he tried again to elicit an admission of guilt and divulgence of the source of the sculpture. The boy went without breakfast.

Apollonius ate his midday meal, drinking noisily from his porridge, making satisfied, smacking sounds upon finishing his pastry—to no avail.

That afternoon, a pair of sharpened chisels were due to be retrieved from the smith, but Apollonius also needed to go by a job site to check measurements for a commission he was bidding. The former task normally would have been entrusted to Myron, for whom visiting the smith was always a treat, but while the boy's stubborn willfulness would serve him well someday, that day had not yet come. Apollonius would have to stop by the smith today himself.

He placed the rabbit on the workbench and, next to it, set a plate with a wedge of cheese, a piece of honeycomb, some almonds and a dried sausage. He informed Myron that he would be welcome to enjoy the food as soon as the rabbit was returned to its rightful owner. It wouldn't even be necessary to reveal where the piece had come from, only that it be returned. Myron's word would be trusted when he had done so, but the task was to be accomplished before Apollonius returned or he himself would take Myron to the magistrate for whatever punishment was due.

The survey of the job-site took longer than Apollonius anticipated, and he had to wait while the smith finished the second chisel. When he returned home, it was near dusk. The rabbit was no longer on the bench. The food was still on the plate.

"Myron?" he called.

The boy was nowhere in sight. Hammurabi was standing in the back doorway, looking into the yard, a low growl rumbling in his throat. There was a scraping sound outside. Apollonius went to investigate.

Sitting on the ground, between the blocks of Parian marble, was the rabbit. Crouched atop one of the blocks, looking down on the rabbit, was a fox. The creature was slinked in a low crouch, its nostrils flared, claws gripping the edge of the block, haunches gathered and coiled as it prepared to launch itself onto its prey. The fur was colored reddish brown, with white on its throat, underbelly, and the tip of its upturned tail. Its dark eyes were gleaming, its upper lip snarled, its bottom lip bared and practically drooling with anticipation. The creature was so lifelike that it might have been breathing. The unsuspecting rabbit below was mere moments from the most trouble it had ever been in. And so was one mischievous boy.

"Myron!"

"Yes, Master?" The muffled reply had come from somewhere in the yard.

"Myron, come here. Now."

Myron stepped slowly out from behind one of the blocks, hands behind his back.

"Did you purchase this?"

"Master, I believe I'm about to pay for it."

"What are you hiding?"

The boy reluctantly brought his hands out from behind his back to reveal a mallet and a chisel. The mallet was Myron's own, an older one that that Apollonius had given him, but the chisel was not one of the chipped, practice tools—it was one of the sculptor's prized chisels from the gift set made by the Alexandrian smith.

"Master, I will buy my own as soon as I have the money to do so. I've only needed to borrow it. The dull ones just wouldn't do . . ." A tear traced down the boy's cheek.

Exasperated, Apollonius marched towards the boy to retrieve the chisel, but he noticed, out of the corner of his eye, behind the marble block, a scattering of limestone chips and the remains of a scrap piece of stone, swept into a pile. One of his good rasps and a file were lying in the dust next to the shop broom, along with several of his pots of paint and two of his brushes.

"I'm cleaning it up, Master." The boy snatched up the broom and began sweeping urgently at the chips.

Apollonius looked from the boy to the fox, from the fox to the rabbit, from the rabbit back to the boy. *It was impossible.* It occurred to him that the clever lad must have set up the elaborate hoax to cover up the theft of the rabbit—by stealing the fox, too, and then making it look as if he himself had . . . because . . . *it was impossible.*

"Give me the broom, Myron."

Myron did so, wincing.

"Come with me."

Myron followed his master into the workshop, chin and lower lip quivering as he watched a low, sturdy worktable being dragged into the middle of the room. Apollonius hefted the broom, frowning, regarding the boy. He left it leaning next to the door on his way back out to the yard. Returning with a fresh block of marble in his arms, he lowered it with a thud in the middle of the worktable. Taking the plate of untouched food, he sat in his chair, propped his feet on a crate and began to eat.

Myron glanced around, confused.

"There you are, young man," Apollonius said, taking a bite off of the end of a sausage and pointing it at the block of stone. "You're welcome to use any and every tool I own. Let's see what you can do."

Myron raised an eyebrow. His other eyebrow rose slowly to match it. "Really, Master?"

"Myron, I don't lie, I don't cheat, and I don't steal, and if you're to continue living under my roof, neither will you. In this household, we earn everything we have, which includes your next meal. Now—let's see what you can do."

Myron looked from the stone to Apollonius, from Apollonius to the row of gleaming tools hanging above the workbench. After a long moment, he approached the bench as would a beggar invited to sit at the king's feast. On his toes, he carefully selected four chisels, two files, a rasp and two mallets, glancing over at Apollonius regularly to ensure that this wasn't a trick, that he wasn't about to get into even more trouble for handling the good tools. He briefly touched the monogrammed mallet from the Alexandrian set, but only to turn it so that its "A" was facing directly outwards.

Apollonius kept eating.

After arranging the implements on the table next to the stone, Myron cleared his throat, wiped his hands on his tunic and looked to Apollonius again.

"What shall I create, Master?"

Apollonius bit off a piece of the cheese. "Whatever you would like, boy. Your favorite thing."

Myron looked down at the marble. He drew in a long, deep breath and released it with a sigh, as if all of the world's worries were washing away. Then he leaned over and kissed the stone.

A tingling raced from Apollonius's scalp to the soles of his feet. He stopped eating.

Picking up the big point chisel and the larger mallet, Myron set to work. Within a half-dozen strikes, he had established the most effective angle of the chisel and the force of the mallet. His rhythm was steady. He increased tempo, moving around the stone with agile fluidity, the chisel following his eye, the mallet following the chisel, his body following the mallet. The chips began flying off of the stone.

The block's top corners disappeared in short order. While maintaining rhythm, Myron would glance over at his master on occasion. Apollonius was trying to maintain the expression of stern displeasure, but it was becoming difficult not to enjoy how much the boy was enjoying himself. It would be a pleasant surprise if the young one could manage to rough out a crude likeness of Hammurabi with the correct number of legs, but Apollonius would have been happy at that point if the boy carved the entire block down to dust without slicing off or mashing a finger.

After finishing the last bit of honeycomb, he settled back and closed his eyes, allowing himself to savor the sound, the steady rhythm of chisel on stone, the separation of the extraneous from the essence—the sound of creation.

He had no intention of teaching Myron how to sculpt. He didn't want a student. It was good enough to have a competent assistant, and there was little harm in letting the boy play with making shapes and helping with the finishing work, but there was no future in sculpting. None. Moreover, there was the risk, the very real danger these days, in creating anything that could be even tangentially associated with paganism. Increasingly, the creation of anything secular at all, or of anything not explicitly Christian, could expose its creator to suspicion and danger. Teaching Myron to sculpt could be a death sentence, and the mere thought of such a demise was more than Apollonius could bear. He had lived through enough loss, enough fleeing from home and having to start over again in strange, foreign places, enough for two or three lifetimes. Myron could become a doctor, or a military officer, or a merchant, or even just a good mason someday. But for now, for this one night, it was okay to let the boy chip away at the stone, to discover for himself that it wasn't so easy. . . .

Apollonius opened his eyes, realizing he had drifted off, apparently for several hours. The sounds of chiseling and filing had stopped. The candles had been lit and had burned well down. Though the evening had cooled considerably, Myron hadn't yet bothered lighting the fire. He was kneeling before what was left of the stone, happily rubbing and polishing away with the emery. Apollonius couldn't see the result, as whatever had been created was facing away from him, if indeed there was a distinguishable front to whatever the thing might be, but from behind, judging by the silhouette of the remaining shape, it appeared to be a head of some sort.

Apollonius stood and stretched. Scratching his beard and reassuming his mien of gruff displeasure, he grumbled and went around to look at the front of the object. Myron paused from his polishing and stepped back to afford his master a view.

What Apollonius saw in the candlelight frightened him very much, but not because the subject itself was in the least frightening. It was a beautifully realized, eerily perfected likeness of—himself. And the likeness wasn't frowning or disapproving at all. It seemed at peace, even happy.

Apollonius looked at the boy, who was studying him with new concern.

"But, Master, you said that I could sculpt my favorite thing. . . ."

Apollonius swallowed and looked away, biting at his inner lip. He looked again at the sculpture and forced himself to try to think, wrinkling his brow.

So he had a sculptor on his hands—a real sculptor—a sculptor who could turn out to be one of the best ever perhaps. And there was nothing he could do about it. Yet he couldn't wrap his mind around what he was seeing or how it had come to be.

"But, Myron, I've taught you *nothing*. . . ."

"But, Master, you've taught me *everything*. I've been watching you. And practicing and practicing in the back when you're away. I wanted to surprise you."

"It's—it's not that easy."

"It's not easy, but simple, really."

"Oh, no, not really—I couldn't do that until I was twice your age, after years of practice, and I was supposedly one of the most gifted—"

"But I always do as you've always told me I should do. I don't just see—I *look*. My eyes measure everything and the relationships between all the parts, and once I've seen it and studied it, I remember things very clearly. Then it's simply a matter of, as you say, Master, freeing it from the stone."

"But Myron, it's not simple—"

"You haven't said whether or not you like it, Master. Do you like it?"

"It's . . . I'm . . . I'm your favorite thing?"

"Of course, Master. And I want to be a sculptor, like you. Will you teach me?"

Apollonius choked back a laugh, blinking away the wetness in his eyes, wondering who would be teaching whom soon enough. He beckoned Myron to stand and he opened his arms. The boy stood hesitantly and stepped into Apollonius's embrace.

"You're not angry, Master?"

"Oh, my dear boy, how can I ever be angry with you?" As Apollonius looked at the portrait, a tear escaped and rolled down his dusty cheek. "Myron, I will teach you all that I know, and you will sculpt gloriously, and the world can be damned. We'll just have to face them together."

Myron drew back and looked up at him askance.

Apollonius wouldn't explain, not tonight. He merely pulled the boy close again.

"But first, we need to get you some food."

He glanced again at the sculpture. The true beauty of it was that what the boy had carved was right: Apollonius was indeed finally at peace, and happy, happier than he had ever been, and he hadn't even realized it. And that was when he knew that his boy was not only a sculptor—but an artist.

Five

APOLLONIUS RUBBED HIS EYES and sat up on the marble block. The town was still too quiet for an early afternoon. The birds had gone silent again. The tenor of the voices in the distance still didn't sound quite right, but having a teenage son—a boy he had come to think of as his son—had been making Apollonius too paranoid of late.

He shuffled his legs to the side of the block and lowered his weight gingerly onto his feet. He called out for Myron, but received no answer. The boy should have returned from the market by now.

He knew that he shouldn't worry as much as he did. He tried not to. Granted, the lad had gotten himself into a couple of brushes with the authorities recently and had experienced a few close scrapes with some rougher types, but it was nearly always due to having spoken the truth, if injudiciously. Courage to speak the truth, and forthrightly, could only be judged as a virtue, but judiciousness in the use of one's tongue was also of much value, particularly for a youth of Myron's age, particularly if he wanted to survive intact to adulthood. Apollonius was trying to teach Myron discretion, but Myron was at a stage in which he saw hypocrisy, injustice and stupidity at every turn, and his indignation was a fiery, spirited horse yet to be bridled—likely he would continue to test the patience of others before achieving the prudence of maturity. It could only be hoped that any lessons the young man had yet to learn wouldn't be too painful or costly.

The old sculptor looked around the yard. He knew each scrap of stone, each chipped slab and busted block, which piece had been part of which project and when. Would he miss this place? He knew he would. Though much pain had been endured here in the beginning, more joy had followed. The limestone rabbit and the fox now lived on opposite ends of the shelf above the workbench inside. The portrait Myron had carved that night had found a home on the mantel above the hearth. While his visage in marble had darkened over the years from the smoke and soot, Apollonius's own days had continued to brighten. Since Myron's appearance at his side on that black night, the days and years had passed quickly, too quickly really, and there was little in the world that still bothered him. There was no changing the past and no value in bemoaning it—he was doing what he loved to do, as well as he could do it. Life was being lived and lived well, all things considered.

Yet there was still the one thing undone. Where once lay two blocks of marble, there remained the one.

He looked at his hands, opening them, turning them over, extending his fingers as far as he was able. The joints were becoming more gnarled, knobbed, less flexible with each passing year. With his eyesight dimming, he wondered how much time he had left. He patted the corner of the marble block, his obdurate old friend and nemesis, and made his way back into the shop.

As it had been in Alexandria, the bronze modello stood on the shelf above the workbench, waiting. He was still unable to put the chisel to the enlargement of it, even now that he could afford the time to do so again, though there had been moments when he thought he was finally seeing, in his mind's eye, the vision of the image he had so long sought, the fulfillment of the promise, the answer to the modello's question, the solution to its suggestion.

Myron would be standing in the doorway, arms crossed, looking out to the horizon with an easy confidence, youthful vigor budding with the calm maturity of a man already tested and proven, or he would have stepped back from one of the works in progress, his eye measuring the composition and the relation of the forms, determining how to proceed, confidently judging the rightness and worthiness of a line, approving the perfection of a hand turned in a gesture just so—and Apollonius would *see* it, at least for a fleeting, evanescent moment. But as quickly and unexpectedly as the vision had appeared, coalescing out of the swirling fog of adolescence, it would dissipate and vanish as the boy lapsed into youthful impatience, distraction and self-doubt. Nonetheless, Apollonius had seen it. He knew it was real. He was sure of it. It was something developing and surfacing in Myron, something for which Apollonius could find no words. It was a pure and powerful amalgam, an alloy of the indomitability of Alexander, the courage of Hercules, the intelligence of Aristotle, the inventiveness of Heron, the passion of Eros. There was a beautiful, heroic, exalted *essence* about the young man, and Apollonius loved it more than anything, perhaps as much as he had loved his Kheimon, and in those moments, he knew that Myron had become *his* favorite thing.

Whatever that essence was, it was all that Apollonius had ever truly been interested in, even when he had been at work creating other things, other subjects, other themes. It was his true passion, the treasure he was always trying to find and to draw forth from the stone. It was all that he himself had ever wanted to be, had ever tried to be, and perhaps had once been, in his youth, before he had seen too much of the world and his soul had been wounded and torn and scattered, never to fully heal. When a man had seen the depths of evil and the horrific ferocity with which men were willing to inflict pain, sorrow, and death upon their fellow beings, how could it be believed that the promise and innocence of youth was anything more than a fleeting illusion, that any purity wasn't doomed by whatever powers that ruled the universe to be defiled and destroyed in the end, as surely as death came eventually to all.

And yet, and yet . . .

He couldn't help but think that Phidias, or whoever had created the modello, had been searching for that very thing, trying to capture it. Maybe there was still hope. If he himself ran out of time and life before he could proceed with the sculpture, he fervently hoped that he wasn't being delusional in believing that Myron might be the one to bring the reality into existence someday. Could the boy's spirit burn cleanly and brightly for long enough to make it so? Could he succeed in living the unwounded, unscarred life? Maybe the Muses required Innocence for the creation of Innocence, as the undamaged, unnicked chisel was needed for carving the clean, unlined plane. Apollonius could hope for nothing more than this for his dear boy. If he had ever wanted to believe in the gods, it would be for just long enough to pray to them to let it be so.

And it was now possible, just possible, that he and Myron might not need the help of the gods after all. They were now on the cusp of finding their own Eden, in the faraway East, in Persia, no less, where the mythical, paradisiacal gardens were said to have been, and perhaps still were. And if there was anything that Apollonius knew with certainty, it was that any garden could be much improved with sculpture.

Yes, life was getting better, and it was about to get a great deal more so, possibly better than he had ever dared hope it could be. As soon as Myron returned, the final decisions could be made, the details arranged. This day could be a momentous day indeed.

As soon as Myron returned . . .

Old Hammurabi was asleep on his pallet, from which he didn't often move these days. An Angora tabby, one of the neighborhood denizens, had stretched languidly across the threshold of the front doorway to lounge in the sun. The world was quiet, too quiet. From somewhere nearby, as the city napped away the heat of the day, a baby began to cry and was hushed by a proffered breast.

Apollonius picked up his file and emery cloth and went back to work on the frieze, smoothing and rounding away the few remaining bumps in the details of the general's breastplate. The work had to be finished by the end of the day, with or without Myron's help, if they were going to be able to leave for the East on the morrow. Apollonius had already alerted the general that the piece would be delivered to the tomb in the morning, that the masons would be paid to install it later.

Hopefully, hopefully, Myron hadn't found trouble again—but in addition to having an imprudent tongue, the young man was also of that age at which boys were easily distracted, and his latest distraction, naturally enough, was a girl. And the girl was the source of Apollonius's present worries.

Over dinner the night before, he had been telling Myron excitedly of the visitor he had received at the shop while Myron had been at the market. The visitor, a rare foreigner in these parts, was wearing a fine turban and silks emblazoned in elegant, eastern motifs. He had introduced himself, in his thick accent, as an envoy representing the interests of a wealthy Sassanid prince, who, having known of Apollonius's reputation from the Alexandrian years, with no little effort and expense had managed to have the sculptor traced to his present location. He had sent his envoy to offer whatever compensation was necessary to have Apollonius moved to Persia to work there for him, permanently and exclusively, being desirous of nothing less than having his palace and grounds filled with sculpture in the classic Greek style. Apollonius was the only one he would have for the position.

It was an astonishing turn of events, an offer so incredible that Apollonius had at first refused to believe it. Surely someone was playing a cruel trick on him. But rather than overtly insulting the envoy in questioning his credibility, Apollonius tactfully protested that he was too old to pull up roots and move so far away, that he couldn't even manage his current projects, at least not without the help of his strong and talented young apprentice—

The envoy had listened patiently, waiting for Apollonius to finish, then insisted that Myron would have to come along as well then, no questions asked, and all the better that there would be such a talented apprentice to carry on the great sculptor's legacy and work after his death. The prince himself was still not old, and he had other palaces. There was several lifetimes' worth of work to be done.

Apollonius thanked the envoy for the prince's generous offer, but explained that he already had commissions lined up for at least the next three years, and—

The envoy had casually uncloaked two heavy purses of gold, as though having anticipated such an objection, and deposited them on the table. The amount was, by far, more than enough for Apollonius to refund the deposits on all scheduled projects and to buy his way out of any and all obligations.

But—could Apollonius take his block of Parian marble?

Of course. The shipping would be arranged without question.

In addition to the generous compensation offered, Apollonius would eat at the prince's table, and he and Myron would be dressed by the prince's tailor. He would be provided with the finest tools and materials—he would need only to request and he would receive. Most remarkable, stirring Apollonius's strongest hopes and doubts, was that the prince was said to be offering him free rein to sculpt whatever subject matter he wished. Moreover, added the envoy, as if tossing in a few amphorae of oil to sweeten and close the deal, Apollonius would be granted his choice of any three women from the prince's personal harem, excluding only the prince's favorite twelve.

Apollonius had laughed with incredulity at this last, but found himself quickly apologizing, gathering from the envoy's dark expression that his response had offended.

Rather than risk further affront by trying to explain that it would be impossible for him to enjoy a woman taken in such a way, much less three of them, he smoothed the moment over, again reminding the envoy of his advancing age. At the very least, he maintained, he would need time to consider the prince's proposal.

The envoy, however, was accustomed to his master's offers being accepted less as proposals and more as inevitabilities. He related, with utmost apology and deference, though his patience was noticeably wearing thin, that his entourage was camped in the hills to the east of town and that he wished to depart without delay. Although he had received the proper permissions from Constantinople to pass through the country, the local garrison had been harassing his caravan and spreading rumors that the Persians were spies. For the older local officers, the last war with the Persians was not a distant memory, and they couldn't see a Persian without envisioning a Persian head on a pike. In addition to suffering the ill will of the garrison, some in the entourage of less hardy constitutions were suffering from the local food and water, and the envoy was desirous of breaking camp as soon as possible. He was willing to grant Apollonius the next day to finish the commission, settle debts and make any necessary arrangements, but he intended to depart by the morning after the morrow, at the latest. He was sure that Apollonius understood and would be able to comply. Expecting no further argument and receiving none, he bowed deeply, turned and walked out of the shop, his silk shoes shushing across the stone floor, his silk robe rippling behind him.

Apollonius had worked for so many years in anonymity, after leaving Alexandria, struggling at times to survive at a level above mere subsistence—and now *this*, and coming at an age at which he was feeling too old to truly take advantage of the opportunity or to fully enjoy it. There were, of course, the lingering doubts. There were too many things that could go wrong, and badly so. It was an extraordinary offer, and all too sudden to be trusted, yet nothing the envoy had said was entirely unreasonable. It was well known that the Persian king was a man of great appetites, and while he wasn't known for appreciating Western art, he was sufficiently liberal that he might allow one of his princes to indulge in such. In Apollonius's judgment, there was much about Eastern art which, though pretty enough by its own standards, hardly qualified as more than decorative craft, with its endlessly repetitive, running motifs, but such was only a purer form of the esthetic now coming into vogue in Constantinople. Could life in the East be any worse than in the West for an artist of Apollonius's leanings?

For young Myron, the Persian mores, manners and language would be more foreign than to Apollonius, who had been exposed to Eastern culture in the melting pot of Alexandria. The food and music would be very different. If Apollonius and Myron were to fall out of favor with their prince for any reason, they would be left completely unprotected. Yet here in the West, with no royal patronage and no blessing from the Church, were they in any less danger? Though he had never heard of this prince, what possible malintent could there be behind such an invitation? The envoy had displayed only the best of courtly manners. He had been attired in the trappings of genuine wealth. Apollonius had been unable to detect the slightest sign of dishonesty or disingenuousness in the man. Surely there was little to lose. Above all, for Myron particularly, there was everything to gain.

Working under the beneficence of a wealthy patron, Apollonius could oversee the completion of Myron's education in anatomy, composition, engineering, esthetics, and mathematics. Western philosophy and science were now being taught in the Eastern courts; good tutors likely would be found there. Myron would have an opportunity to flourish in the East, to become as great an artist as his ambition allowed and desired. He might even be allowed to sculpt heroic, grand-scale subjects and themes without fear of persecution. The world could be remade in his image. . . .

Over dinner, as Apollonius enthusiastically described the prospects for the future, his voice quickening with near giddiness, he realized that Myron was barely listening. The boy was gazing off into the distance, his face nearly expressionless. He was barely touching his food.

"Tell me, what is the matter, Myron?"

Myron didn't answer. He shifted uncomfortably in his seat, his lips pursed.

"I can understand," Apollonius offered, mustering his patience, "how you might be hesitant to leave here. After all, this town is the only home you've ever known, and going off to a completely foreign place where you don't know anyone or have any friends or—"

"I can't go," the boy sighed.

"What do you mean, you can't go?"

Myron would only shake his head. It took Apollonius half an hour to pry out of him that the problem was a girl, a girl Myron had met only the day before yet was completely smitten with, a girl who was the source of the blue silk sash wound through his belt. After more prying and cajoling, Myron finally confessed, the words spilling and tumbling out of him, that she was the most beautiful, most enchanting, most intelligent, most beguiling, most fascinating creature he had ever laid eyes on, and as far as leaving for Persia the day after tomorrow, he didn't want to go, he couldn't go, he wouldn't go.

Apollonius understood, though he wished he didn't. Coaxing, explaining, trying to convince Myron that he would meet so many wonderful, exotically gorgeous girls in the East was, of course, to no effect. Nothing would budge him. Apollonius's arguments weren't much better than half-hearted anyway: he knew what it was to be in love, and admittedly, having not met the girl himself, he could hardly argue that the attraction was mere youthful infatuation. Was it inconceivable that, at a young age, Myron may have already met his own Kheimon? How wonderful would that be? How might Apollonius's own life have been different, had only . . . ? But his own spring and summer had passed. The future was Myron's now.

So the girl was a problem, and a rather serious one. Apollonius knew that any hope of an opportunity such as the prince's offer ever coming again was beyond all odds, beyond consideration. Myron's career, his life and livelihood likely depended on decisions that would have to be made over the next few hour's time.

Apollonius had delved further. Did Myron know where the girl came from? No. Did he know how long this traveling family would be staying in town? No. The girl was probably too young to marry. They couldn't just kidnap her and throw her in a bag and haul her off to Persia—though the musing drew a sidelong smile from

Myron, which Apollonius counted as a small victory. Might she be purchased? Based on Myron's description of her sales skills, she was likely an invaluable asset to the family's business, and as most daughters would be, she was probably more loved than not—they wouldn't let her go easily or cheaply. Apollonius eyed the purses of Persian gold on the workbench, wondering how much he might be able to afford for her after clearing his other obligations. But then, buying the girl would be no better for Myron than taking a woman from the prince's harem would be for Apollonius.

On being pressed, Myron had to admit that he couldn't know if the girl would be willing to leave her family and go with him to Persia, or if she wouldn't.

The boy was near tears of frustration, head in his hands, fingers in his hair. Apollonius eased the interrogation, promising they could sleep on it. Perhaps they would think of a solution by morning. They retired to their beds in the loft.

An hour after having blown out the lamp, Apollonius finally settled on a way to proceed. Myron was still awake, tossing and turning, his nose buried in the silk sash, sighing fitfully. Apollonius suggested that in the morning Myron should go and tell the girl about needing to move to Persia, and that if she wanted to go too, they should try to get her father's permission, and immediately. If her father raised the matter of compensation, it would have to be dealt with, but first, it should be determined whether the girl would even want to go at all, and then if so, if her father would allow it under any circumstances. It was a reasonable first step, to which Myron agreed, though not without anxiety.

Apollonius fell asleep, his mind at ease, to dream of an endless field of gently rolling hills beneath a cloudless sky. In rows extending as far as the eye could see stood blocks of quarried marble in every conceivable dimension and size. In their midst rose an enormous monolith of virgin stone as tall as a pyramid, as wide as a town square. His mallet and chisel at the ready, Apollonius circled the monolith's base, examining it, trying to decide where to start. The stone was so pure, there wasn't a flaw or vein to be found in it. As he walked, youthfully, agelessly, his eyesight sharp, his body strong and free of pain, he kept an eye out for whoever was surely about to appear to tell him what he could create from the marble, or what he couldn't—but there was no one. He was alone and free to do as he pleased. It was heaven.

He rounded a corner and found his Kheimon sitting next to the monolith's wall on a blanket spread with a feast of delectable food she had prepared. He sat and they ate and drank and laughed like children at the opportunity before him. When she smiled, her eyes danced with the joy of a young girl, a girl in a blue sash who sold fabric from a tent in the marketplace. . . .

The next morning, Apollonius was buoyant of spirit and eager with anticipation. Myron was miserable. Judging by the boy's glazed eyes and the darkness beneath them, he hadn't slept at all; yet, after finishing his morning chores, he washed, changed into a clean tunic and, with his brow set determinedly, marched off to the market, the blue sash tied about his arm.

Apollonius blew the marble dust from the crevices of the general's breastplate and laid his file aside. The finishing work would go faster later, with Myron's help and good vision. He wondered what could be keeping the boy. Perhaps the young doves were still trying to raise the courage to proposition her father. Perhaps they were still trying to decide how best to go about doing so, or perhaps they had already approached him and reaped an angry refusal and had run off to commiserate and decide what course of action to follow. Perhaps, and not unlikely, the girl didn't want to go to Persia at all. If not, hopefully Myron would be mature enough to grasp the importance of pursuing his career, relative to the value of spending a few more days or weeks with a girl who would be moving along to the next town soon enough anyway. Apollonius was bracing for an angry, stubborn argument upon the boy's return. In the meantime, he could waste no more time getting their affairs in order.

From the door, he looked up and down the street. Myron was still nowhere to be seen. A number of townspeople were making their way in the direction of the square. When they noticed the sculptor, it seemed as though they looked away rather too quickly. He called out cheerfully to Ioannes the carpenter, with whom he had worked on a number of projects, but Ioannes kept walking, passing without acknowledging Apollonius's greeting, staring straight ahead. He was carrying one of his large hammers. Apollonius called out again, more loudly. Ioannes half-turned, ducking his head to mutter a furtive reply before quickening his pace.

The old hollowness reappeared in Apollonius's stomach. He tried not to read too much into it. It could have been anything. Maybe Ioannes was cheating on his wife and thought perhaps Apollonius had learned of it, or maybe he had lost some teeth and was embarrassed to have people notice. Any of a dozen explanations could be as plausible. One should never assume the worst except from the worst, as he was fond of telling Myron.

He pulled the door shut and retreated to the westerly corner of the shop. Maneuvering a heavy, unfinished sculpture of a centaur out of position, he uncovered a dust-free rectangle of floor. After ensuring that no one had come in after him or was peering through the windows, he knelt and lifted away several unsecured boards. The hollowed space below was dug out to be just large enough to fit Myron and himself. Years ago, he had trained the boy to climb down into the space as quickly and silently as possible and to pull the boards back in place over him. Then he had made Myron lie silently in the hole for the better part of a day to ensure that, in an emergency, the boy could remain disciplined and quiet and not succumb to panic. The hole also served as their treasury, where a few bags of gold coin were kept. To the modest cache, he now added one of the purses given to him by the envoy, keeping the second purse out for settling accounts that afternoon. The balance would be retrieved when they were ready to leave the next morning.

At the sound of running feet and the repeated calling of his name, he hurriedly replaced the boards, slipping the last one back into place just as a young boy dashed into the shop breathlessly, the door banging loudly behind him, which set Hammurabi to barking.

"Apollonius! Apollonius! Come quickly!" It was Attalus, the dark-haired urchin who ran everywhere and had more questions than anyone in town could possibly answer.

"What's wrong, Attalus?" His first thought was for Myron.

"There's a stranger at the fountain, and he was looking at it for a long time, and he asked me if I knew who made it, and I said 'yes,' and he said he wants to meet you—" he took a breath—"and so you need to go and meet him."

"Was the man wearing a cloth wrapped around his head? Was he wearing silk slippers?"

"No, sir. He doesn't have any hair. His head naked."

Apollonius considered it for a moment, then chuckled at the irony. First the Persian envoy, and now, the very next day, someone who might be interested in commissioning a larger work, just as Apollonius was readying to leave town. Over his career, it seemed that it had been ever thus: too little work for long stretches, followed by more work than he could handle. The waves and troughs. He dug into his purse and gave the boy a coin.

"Attalus, run and ask the man nicely if he would come here to the shop. I'm very busy today, and you know I don't walk as quickly or easily anymore."

"Yes, sir!" The boy turned and ran toward the door.

"Attalus!"

The boy skidded to a stop. "Yes, sir?"

"If you see Myron, please tell him that I need for him to come home right away."

"Yes, sir!"

"And don't slam the—"

But the door was already reverberating from its concussion with the wall, which started Hammurabi to barking again.

Six

"APOLLONIUS! SIR! The man says he will not come to the shop. He wants you to come to the fountain! I think he's a very important man. There are people around him who move their heads up and down a lot when he talks."

Apollonius sighed. Another important man with an entourage. He didn't have time for it, not today, but his professionalism and experience wouldn't allow him to ignore a potential customer, regardless how eccentric or demanding. And what if Myron refused to go to Persia? What then? The prospect of another big commission, possibly another large fountain somewhere in the region, could not yet be dismissed.

Attalus was tugging anxiously at his arm. Apollonius followed as quickly as he was able, which wasn't quickly at all, out of the shop and toward the square, wincing at the uneven paving stones beneath his aching feet.

The fountain had been the first major project that he and Myron had worked on together. The summer prior to its creation, he had taken the boy to Constantinople to see the trove of grand sculpture that had been confiscated by Constantine and the successive Christian emperors, taken from the reaches of the empire. The magnificent, iconic artworks of civilization, once revered and treasured, had been removed from their sheltering temples and brought to the capital to be put on public display, reduced to the status of so many shackled prisoners of war, to be exposed to the elements and held up for the public's entertainment and scorn. Scattered in and around the Great Palace, the Hippodrome, and the Senate were the spoils of conquered culture: the famous tripods from Delphi, the Zeus from Dodona, the Athena from Lindos, the Heracles by Lysippos, Romulus and Remus with their she-wolf, the four gilded horses from Chios, the Delphian Serpent Column of the Plataean tripod, the Aphrodite of Cnidos by Praxiteles, and Phidias' great chryselephantine Zeus from Olympia. In the baths of Zeuxippos alone were some eighty antique bronzes. Countless other masterpieces were held in the palaces and private mansions of the city. The Roman tradition of parading conquered foes and plunder through the capital had evolved to a deeper, more philosophic level with the Christian emperors, who understood the power of symbols and icons and treated the idols of their vanquished competitors accordingly.

The visit to Constantinople effected an immediate change on Myron, maturing and sobering the young man as he absorbed and studied the creations of the great masters long dead. After several days of touring, studying, and discussing art history and technique, Apollonius took him to see the chariot races in the Hippodrome, to lighten the mood.

As they approached the stadium's entrance, the crowd parted for the emperor's parade of musicians, mounted guards, and two pair of lumbering, richly bedecked elephants. Myron studied the behemoths with intent interest. After the races, while passing through one of the city's markets, they passed a small herd of antelope tied in a pen, offered as exotic pets. A year later, when designing and sculpting the fountain, Apollonius barely remembered having seen the antelope, but Myron, apparently, had absorbed the structure and detail of the animals' form in a matter of minutes; he was able to recreate them in life-like detail, as he did the family of elephants.

The fountain had come as a commission from Valerius, the retired governor of the province, at whose villa Apollonius had done extensive restoration work. The old patrician was beyond wealthy, and in the twilight of his life he had endeavored to recreate, in the quiet backwater where he had retired, something of the glory of Rome. His villa could have been lifted out of the Italian countryside. He had taken pride in patronizing and promoting Apollonius's work over the years, claiming to anyone who would listen that it was he himself who had re-discovered Apollonius, rescuing the genius from obscurity. When it was the ailing man's desire to fund a fountain for the town, to leave a legacy reminiscent of those in the Italian cities and villages of his youth, Apollonius was, of course, the only choice for producing it.

The town elders had accepted the governor's generosity without question or reservation. They wouldn't have thought to insult the esteemed and powerful patrician by asking what the subject of the fountain would be. It wouldn't have crossed anyone's mind to assume that a man of such established taste and propriety would provide anything less than the most appropriate of subjects. Valerius, in turn, had given Apollonius free rein to create whatever subject matter his heart desired, with no expense to be spared.

Three local masons and two strong helpers were hired as assistants, and with Myron's full participation and partnership, Apollonius had set about designing and sculpting what would become the town's centerpiece, replacing the crumbling stone bowl that had served the community's needs for centuries. The masons constructed the ascending pools, along with the fountain's steps, columns, the plumbing and embellishments, while Myron worked on creating the animals and Apollonius focused his own efforts on the human figures. For the central figure to grace the fountain's top, one of the long-reserved blocks of Parian marble was dedicated: its time had come, or more accurately, Apollonius was finally ready to release the image he had long seen within it. He wanted Myron to see her. He was ready for the world to see her. Most of all, he himself wanted and needed for her to exist.

During the early phases of construction, a number of the more prominent townspeople, particularly the Church elders, began to express skepticism and concern:

What are these? Elephants? There's never been an elephant within a hundred leagues of this town! What is this about? If we wanted a circus, we would build a coliseum. Shouldn't the central figure be the emperor Theodosius, or the archbishop Proclus, or our town's beloved patron, Saint Helena? Those girls are hardly wearing enough clothes—look at their bare knees! It's an outrage. Such rank immodesty sets a poor example for the youth. And those funny looking, skinny goat-things standing by the elephants—what are those supposed to be? They wouldn't feed a mouse's family—they're bad luck. God will curse us with famine next year, mark my word. . . .

Apollonius was deaf to the niggling chatter, and
Valerius would hear no complaints, protecting his artist
from any and all charges and from demands for changes.
As the fountain neared completion and grew in popularity,
particularly among the children of the town, the grumblings
and snide asides of the adults gradually diminished. Indeed,
most of the townspeople came to fall in love with their
new centerpiece and landmark, showing it off proudly to
visiting relatives and to every traveler passing through.

At the ceremony celebrating the completion of the
project, the water was re-diverted, and as it began to flow
through the boys' amphorae and the elephants' trunks,
Valerius wept with joy, declaring Apollonius's creation
to be, if not as large or complex as some in Rome, the
most beautiful yet and as elegant as any ever created. He
sponsored a three-day festival in celebration, with the
fountain as the event's centerpiece, at which the entire town
was dined and wined to satiety. Poems to the fountain's
beauty were composed and read. The children sang a
chorus in appreciation of Valerius. The region's best actors
were engaged to recite, using the fountain's rim as a stage,
soliloquies from the classic dramas of antiquity.

While Valerius himself, in his speech, gave praise
and recognition to Apollonius, the speakers following
him mentioned Valerius only, for his vision and gracious
beneficence. As mere apprentice, Myron was not referenced
once in the proceedings, but the lack of recognition could
not have mattered less to him. He was absorbed with other
concerns, the most pressing of which was a trio of girls,
two of whom were twin sisters, following him around,
bringing him food and drink, competing coquettishly for
his attentions. They begged and cajoled him into dancing

with them—to which he finally relented, though he would only do so with all three at once, for efficiency. By the end of the feast's second day, they were proving unshakeable. Using the excuse of needing to relieve himself, he ducked behind a bush, climbed a garden wall and took the back alleys to the shop, where without so much as lighting a candle to reveal his location, he climbed to the loft for precious sleep and solitude.

Valerius, ever known for his timing and sense of decorum, having secured his legacy for the ages, saw fit to pass away peacefully in his sleep the evening following the feast's conclusion. The town elders engaged one of the masons to engrave a short appreciation to their benefactor on the fountain's rim.

It seemed that everyone had a different name and story for the lady gracing the fountain, declaring her to be either this mythical goddess or that great queen or a character from one of the Jewish or Christian tales. Several of the elders were convinced that the woman was Jesus' mother herself. Others proclaimed, as they had expected and insisted all along, that she was Saint Helena, mother of Constantine, who had slept for an evening in the town on her return from having discovered the True Cross in Jerusalem. There was already a shrine to Helena on the one side of the square—it was the only obvious choice. Other ancient and previously unknown myths behind the fountain's story materialized from the ether and were embellished with each retelling, as those championing the tales competed to have their version be the one to survive and be passed down through future generations.

But Apollonius would address no speculation, would answer no question as to the figure's identity or the fountain's theme. He allowed everyone to enjoy her for what they would. As for himself, whenever he passed her on his way to the market, he would look up and be content in his own reveries. It was rumored that sometimes, late on the warm summer nights, the old sculptor could be seen lying on the fountain's upper rim, his fingers intertwined on his chest, seemingly having a conversation with no one but himself, while gazing at the constellations turning through the heavens above. He would stay, it was said, some nights until dawn. And whether he had been seen in the square the night before or not, the townspeople would always find, each morning, a fresh blue lotus flower lying at the fountain's base, though lotus flowers were difficult and quite expensive to obtain so far north of Egypt.

☙

It wasn't a soft summer's night and there were no constellations turning above when Attalus pulled Apollonius into the square. The afternoon's heat was oppressive. The sun baked the paving stones.

Apollonius stopped. For the third time in as many hours, he sensed something amiss. From the direction of the fountain, which given his failing vision was only a hazy blur, a fervent, sonorous litany could be heard, a voice rolling and carrying to the surrounding buildings, filling the square and echoing back to the center. Other voices filled the speaker's measured pauses with affirmation, mixed with the occasional snorting of horses and what sounded like the clinking of metal hardware or armor. With no little reluctance, Apollonius allowed Attalus to lead him closer, and the edges of the masses began to define.

The crowd was pressing forward to listen to a man standing against the rim of the fountain's lower bowl. As he spoke, he gestured from the people to the sky above, and from the fountain to the earth below. Positioned unobtrusively nearby, monitoring with impatient boredom, were six mounted soldiers from the local garrison, accompanied by a dozen foot soldiers in loose formation, shifting uncomfortably in the heat. Apollonius couldn't imagine what exigency could require so many soldiers— the crowd seemed peaceable enough, and while the tone of the speaker seemed serious, there was no hint of riot in the air. He couldn't recall there ever having been a riot in the town, unlike in Alexandria, where mobs and riots had been as common and regular as sandstorms in the spring.

He squinted to make out Ioannes. The carpenter, standing at the back of the crowd, was listening intently, and still holding his hammer. The town's baker was nearby, as was the blacksmith and his portly wife. Apollonius recognized several of the Armenian washerwomen from the river and the seamstress who mended his clothing, along with her pretty daughter. Apollonius gave the girl his customary wink—she always had a shy smile for him in return. But today, she looked away. Several of the farmers and herdsmen from the market were present, as were the shoemaker, two of the fullers, the apprentice to the jeweler, and the bent old poet from Crete. These were all neighbors and acquaintances. Some could be counted as friends. There might have been two or three hundred or more present. The town's paunchy prefect, in his striped magisterial toga, stood next to the speaker, a bound volume tucked under his arm.

Gathered near the speaker and the prefect was a collective of unshaven men in undyed robes. The ascetic monks typically emerged from their caves and grottos in the hills only a few times a year, to come into town for supplies. They never lingered. Seeing them in the square, next to his fountain, made Apollonius's breath quicken and his pulse begin to throb. They were too close to her.

He looked around for Myron, half expecting to see the boy collared by one of the soldiers. As impatient as he had been earlier for Myron's return, he now hoped the boy was lingering somewhere on the far side of town, in an alley kissing the girl perhaps, and if so, that the girl would remain willing awhile longer.

He still couldn't discern the man's words, nor did he have a clear view of the fellow. "Who is it?" he asked an elderly woman at the rear of the crowd.

She looked at him askance, frowning. "Weren't you in church today? Why, that is the new bishop!"

Apollonius grimaced. He allowed Attalus to make way for them, through the rear rows, until the bishop's words became intelligible—

"And God asks the people of this place: 'Has it been so long since I brought you out from the darkness? Is it not enough that I spilled the blood of my only son and gave his body to save you from the wickedness you were born into?'"

"It is enough," murmured several in reply.

"And yet," the bishop's voice rose angrily, "when the one and only God above, who has saved you from your sinful nature, sends his humble messenger to you today, it is only to find that in your pride and haughtiness you have returned to the ways of old, making a mockery of his eternal grace, his patience, his forgiveness, and the gift of his son's blood."

The people stood in silent contriteness, many with bowed heads. Apollonius now had a clear view of the man's face: there was something in the voice, in the manner, in the chinless jaw line that was disturbingly familiar. He edged his way closer yet for a clearer view.

"And is it not written, 'You shall make no idols nor graven images, nor raise a standing image, nor shall you set up any image of stone in your land to bow down unto it, for I am the Lord your God'"?

"Yes, yes, it is written!" came the penitent reply.

The bishop pointed an accusatory, trembling finger at the figure atop the fountain. All heads now bowed. The townspeople could not bear to lift their eyes to look at the object they had loved but was now the source of their shame. As the bishop scanned the town's inhabitants, his gaze seeming to fall upon each and every one of them. He did not fail to notice the one man in the crowd whose head remained unbowed, whose eyes remained fixed steadily on his own. He noted as well the boy Attalus holding the man by the sleeve. Studying Apollonius, he continued speaking, his voice cutting to the hearts of his audience.

"And did not your God engrave this very commandment in stone: 'You shall have no other gods before me. You shall not make any graven image, or any likeness of any thing that is in heaven above, or that is in the earth beneath, or that is in the water under the earth. You shall not bow down thyself to them, nor serve them, for I, the Lord thy God, am a jealous God'"?

Utter silence had fallen on the square. The citizenry were shifting uncomfortably. The bishop offered them no relief. As some began to hope that the worst of the remonstrations had passed, they peered up from beneath their bowed brows. Seeing that the bishop's wrath was focused on a particular person in the crowd, someone other than themselves, they began searching for the subject of his attention.

The bishop's glare shifted between Apollonius and the figure atop the fountain. A thin curl began to pull at the side of his mouth.

"Are *you* the man who created this?" he demanded.

In a strong, steady voice, Apollonius answered, "I am."

The crowd parted, opening a path between them. Attalus let go of Apollonius's sleeve and took shelter behind the apron of the butcher's wife.

Apollonius was now certain of it: the man was Peter, Peter the Reader, once the Nitrian monk, once deacon and assistant to Cyril of Alexandria.

The bishop again studied the fountain and again turned to Apollonius.

"The woman, she looks—familiar."

"You didn't know her," Apollonius replied.

Several in the crowd murmured at the evident lack of contriteness and respect.

The bishop noticed the blue lotus flower at the base of the fountain, lying next to a white lily. He bent to pick it up. The flower of the Nile had begun to wilt in the heat. Turning it over thoughtfully in his hand, he began plucking the petals, deliberately, one by one, watching Apollonius's face as he did so.

"Are you, or are you not, Apollonius of Alexandria?" he asked.

One of the horses pawed nervously at the pavement. The foot soldiers stopped fidgeting and came to order, sensing the change in the air. The contingent's captain turned his horse toward the crowd and held it on short rein.

Apollonius watched as Peter crushed what remained of the flower in his fist and tossed it casually into the pool.

◌♥

To Peter, and to all in Alexandria other than Apollonius, the teacher whom Apollonius had been invited to call Kheimon had been known by her given name—Hypatia, daughter of the scholar Theon. Her father had been one of the last remaining members of the Museum before the vestiges of the great library and school were destroyed by the Nitrian monks. He had survived to teach his daughter everything he knew of mathematics, astronomy and philosophy. Hypatia, in turn, surpassed her father in eruditeness and learning to become, by no design of her own, one of the most respected, admired, and sought-after scholars in the western world.

When Cyril arrived in Alexandria, as the new bishop, his ambition was to rule the city by God's law, or by his interpretation of it, and he loathed and envied Hypatia for her popularity and influence with the civil authorities. Not only was she a *woman*, but an unbowed, unrepentant *pagan*. He could hardly speak her name without spitting it.

The morning after she had brought her students to visit Apollonius's workshop, sectarian rioting erupted once again in the city, fueled by the power struggle between the bishop Cyril and the city's prefect, Orestes. Throughout the conflict, Hypatia stood on the side of Orestes, brilliantly and persuasively defending the rule of civil law, to Cyril's fury.

And it was thus, on a crisp March day during the season of Lent, as Hypatia was on her way home from the school, that her chariot was ambushed and stopped by Peter the Reader and his associates, the Nitrian monks.

ೞ

Apollonius watched what was left of the crushed lotus drifting toward the fountain's center, caught in a slow-moving eddy, the water gurgling and tumbling as prettily as it had on the fountain's first day. Peter nodded to the prefect who, turning to face those gathered, opened his codex. With shaking fingers, he fumbled through the parchment pages, searching for the place he had marked.

It hadn't escaped Apollonius's attention that two of the soldiers had been shifting around to the rear of the crowd and were now stopped directly behind him. He motioned for Attalus. Bending low, he whispered in the boy's ear, insisting that Attalus repeat the message back. He pressed a coin into the boy's hand and gave him a pat, sending him on his way. Attalus bolted through the rear of the crowd, dodging the soldiers' attempt to grab him.

At the bishop's signal, the soldiers advanced. Taking Apollonius by the arms, they ushered him forward. The monks parted to let them through. Apollonius wrinkled his nose—he had forgotten how bad the unwashed ascetics smelled. The prefect, the same who had proudly presided over the fountain's opening, had found the page he was looking for. His mouth dry, he motioned for a drink from his assistant's flask, then clearing his throat, he began to read aloud from the law.

Seven

MYRON RETURNED TO THE WORKSHOP to find Apollonius absent and Hammurabi lying awake on his pallet, head on his paws, whimpering. Myron gave him a few scratches between the ears.

It had been a turbulent, exhilarating morning. The absence of his master, who had left no note as to where he had gone or for how long he would be away, was causing the apprentice almost unbearable frustration. He had never been long on patience anyway.

At the market, Myron had waited until Sira's mother wasn't looking, and slipping out from behind the urn merchant's stall, he caught Sira's eye and beckoned to her. Leaving her mother in charge, she followed him into a close, shadowed alley. It was the first time they had been alone together.

Myron had never been much of a salesman. He had been told by Apollonius that, if he wanted to survive in the business world, he needed to learn how to properly present himself and his work to prospective employers, to learn how to negotiate a good price; so far, Myron's sales skills amounted to accepting whatever someone was willing to pay for whatever they wanted. As long as he could eat and work, he was happy.

But today, he needed to sell, and he dug deep. He had seen and heard people doing this kind of thing before, of course, especially in the market. Apollonius was very good at negotiating. Sira was a natural at establishing relationships with her buyers. Could Myron sell to an expert seller? He would give it his best effort. Above all, he was determined to remain honest. He couldn't bear the thought of tricking Sira into doing something she might later regret.

He had her to himself. The alley was otherwise deserted. He stepped back and, with one look at her, forgot all about selling.

"What are you doing?" she asked, laughing.

"Measuring . . ." he said distractedly, his eyes scanning and tracing her figure from head to foot, hand to elbow, elbow to shoulder, across the shoulders, from the crown of her head to the bottom of her chin to the hollow of her throat, to her waist, across her hips, the length of her thigh. "The clothes are in the way. . . ."

She flushed and glanced around, alarmed. "*What?* Not here—"

"Not here. But if you're going to be my model, I'll need to see you nude, of course. From all angles. Different positions . . ." He was shifting around behind her to examine her backside, to which she turned and kept turning, to remain facing him.

"This works both ways, you know," she said, looking up and down his body, measuring him in turn. "If I'm to dress you properly, you won't be able to keep those rags on."

He was studying the distance between her eyes, the angle between the corners of her mouth and the edges of her nose, the curve of her lips—lingering on her lips. "What's wrong with what I'm wearing?"

She took the frayed edge of his threadbare sleeve between her fingers. "Really, Myron, this won't do at all. Not for *my* sculptor. I have a reputation to maintain, you know."

"Just how far does your reputation extend?" He took her hands in his and told her all about the Persian envoy, about the opportunity being offered to him and Apollonius in the East, how exciting life might be in such an exotic place. For her benefit he described, as best as he remembered Apollonius telling it, the fine silks the envoy had been wearing.

She responded excitedly with what she had heard of the luxurious fabrics and designs in fashion in the Eastern courts. "How wonderful it would be for you to visit and work there," she said wistfully.

"I would like to go—but I can't go. Not without you, Sira."

She leaned in and kissed him on the cheek. He, in turn, kissed her on the lips.

When she stopped blinking, she said, "You absolutely *must* go, Myron. It would be foolish not to."

"I absolutely *will not* go, not without my muse and model." He kissed her again. She kissed him back.

She thought about it for a moment, then declared matter-of-factly, "Okay then. Let's go."

He stood staring at her. "But, we'll have to ask your father—won't we?"

"We probably should."

"But he'll say no—won't he?"

"He'll be furious. He won't let me go."

Myron hesitated, feeling it was indecent to make the suggestion. He fumbled through it anyway: "My master has money. How much do you think . . . ?"

She laughed. "Your master doesn't have enough money. It's been tried before. It happens rather often actually."

Myron flushed angrily, experiencing jealousy for the first time in his life and not enjoying it in the least.

"But you would go with me," he asked, "even if your father forbade it?"

"Oh yes."

A shadow crossed his countenance.

"Oh, don't worry about them," she said. "My family will be fine without me. They've been doing this all their lives, long before I came along, and frankly, they've been getting pretty lazy lately, with me around."

"Oh, I'm not worried—if you're not."

"I'm not worried. By the way, leave the selling to me. You do the sculpting, I'll make you famous the world over, and we'll be as rich as kings before you know it."

He threw his head back and laughed. He *loved* this girl! And though he didn't come out and say it, he was rather proud of his sales skills: after all, he was leaving with what he came for.

He drew her close and they kissed again, tentatively, awkwardly, then daring to hold their lips together longer. She felt his hand brush the side of her face on the way to the back of her neck. His hand cradled her head, holding her mouth to his. Her lips parted. She melted into him. Her future was sealed.

The young lovers released, gasping, catching their breath. They kissed once more and agreed that she should pack a few necessities that evening. She would leave a note for her parents and meet him at the fountain at midnight.

"Let's go then," he said, hardly believing his fortune.

"Yes, let's go." Her eyes shone, flashing.

He hesitated, holding her hands a moment longer.

"One more thing—" he said.

"Yes?"

"Sira . . ."

"Yes?"

"Sira . . ."

"Myron?"

"I just love the sound of your name. *Sira . . .*"

ᘓ

Myron paced in the workshop, awaiting his master's return, unsure where to start with the preparations for departure. Though he knew there was a great deal to be done, the prospect was entirely overwhelming. How much could they take with them? How would they take it? How much would be left here and what would happen to it? Where to begin? Apollonius would know.

The street outside seemed unusually quiet and empty. Only the cats and dogs were about, and all but Hammurabi were still taking their midday naps. Hammurabi would have to come with them, of course. Myron wondered how far the old boy would be able to walk on his own. They would have to make room for him in a wagon.

He noticed that the sculpture of the centaur had been moved, but that the floorboards, though exposed, were still in place. Worried that someone may have robbed them, seeing one of the new purses of coin in clear view on the workbench, he lifted the boards and confirmed that their gold was still cached below. Apollonius must have absentmindedly left the one purse out. Myron added it to the others in the hole. He stared down into the darkness before replacing the board.

He hated that hole. He hadn't known how miserable it could be to be trapped in a tight, close space until Apollonius had made him lie there silently in the darkness for hours on end with nothing but slivers of light and dust filtering down from between the boards. Younger then, he had been so panicked by the experience that he cried through most of it, as silently as he could manage, trying to be brave and wanting desperately not to disappoint his master.

Though the existence of the hole and the other emergency plans and preparations seemed quite important to Apollonius, to Myron it all seemed rather paranoid and overwrought. It was hard to blame the old man, given what he had been through first in Greece, then in Alexandria. Apollonius hadn't spoken of those times often or in much detail, but when he had, he had related enough that Myron was convinced there were some very evil and dangerous people in the world, and that one shouldn't be complacent. Myron had been taught that it was so and he knew the lessons well, at least in his head, though in his heart it was impossible to believe that anything so bad could ever happen to them here, not in this peaceful town in the middle of nowhere, not in their home, where they had so many friends and were now quite popular and respected for having created the town's pride and joy, the fountain. Of real violence, Myron had never witnessed more than a few fistfights and the public flogging of a thief.

He wondered, now that he was older and twice the size he had been when Apollonius had first put him through the emergency training, how much more claustrophobic the hole would feel. He shuddered at the thought of it. And with both him and Apollonius wedged into the hole together? Would they even fit? It was almost unthinkable, and another reason to be happy they were leaving. Myron wouldn't miss the hole. If Apollonius insisted on having another one dug wherever they were going, Myron would make sure that it was dug large enough to fit four elephants—and he'd devise a way of putting a window in it.

He thought he should start packing the tools, at least, but wasn't sure what Apollonius would want left out for finishing the commission. He scanned the sets of chisels, files and mallets, hoping that a good smith could be found in Persia. Apollonius claimed that it had taken him three years to properly train the one here in town.

He greeted the modello on the shelf above, asking aloud if it was ready for another adventure, a journey to yet another new land.

He couldn't recall when he had started talking to it. He didn't have a name for the man. Over the years, his master had shared everything he knew and speculated about the modello, what he believed it represented. As pleased as Apollonius was with the rendering of the sculpture atop the fountain, it was the enlargement of the modello which remained the first and ultimate desire of his heart. Though he had told no one in town but Myron, whom he had sworn to secrecy, Apollonius hoped someday to create the male counterpart to Kheimon and raise it on a pedestal on the side of the square facing her. She was already looking at him, or at least at the place where he would be, as he would be looking at her.

The desire and intent to bring the object into existence was as personal to Apollonius as a thing could be, and Myron, as he grew older, thought that he was beginning to understand. The master and apprentice would sit for hours of the evenings, the modello on its shelf lit by the flickering light from the fire. Apollonius would talk of the ancient philosophers' views of Man, of Man's nature and his place in the universe. Some evenings, Apollonius would be studying the modello without saying anything at all and, closing his eyes, his hands would begin to move through the air, shaping, carving, shifting the masses, extending the lines, tightening the forms, refining the features, adjusting the pose. The next morning, he would have Myron bring some clay up from the river, and with much optimism, he would begin the forming, starting at a scale only twice that of the modello. But with each attempt, in exhausted frustration, he would end up destroying what he had built, pushing and punching the clay back down into an amorphous lump. It could be months, sometimes a year or more, before he would attempt it again.

Myron himself never touched the modello, but when Apollonius wasn't around, he would converse with it, about everything and anything that was important to him, as he had seen the younger girls talking with the stick figures they would dress up. Apollonius said that to know oneself would be to know what the statue would be, and that to see the statue would be to know what a man could be. Myron thought it might be best to get to know the sculpted man from the inside out—working opposite his master's approach. And to know the man, he would first let the man get to know him. It seemed only fair, and hopefully practical. And so he talked to the modello, and found that the more he talked, the more he got to know himself. He was increasingly confident that, someday, if Apollonius hadn't already done so, he himself would learn just who the man was, and then he would bring him to life. Larger than life. Much larger.

The modello was almost a third person in their relationship, their own secret obsession, though they never spoke of it as such. It was simply a thing that had come to be understood, a part of them. The fulfillment of the modello's promise was the eventuality on the horizon which had to be done, and would be done, as surely as they both breathed. Myron felt certain that Sira, too, would understand. There was something in the way she looked at him that was exactly the way Apollonius looked at the modello. The way she watched Myron, the way she listened to him, gave him the freedom to talk with her as easily as he talked with—

Attalus ran in, out of breath, his chest heaving, eyes wide.

"Myron! Apollonius—"

"Apollonius isn't here, Attalus. What's wrong?"

"I know he's not here, Myron. He's at the fountain. He told me . . . to tell you . . ."

Attalus stopped to catch his breath, bending over, hands on his knees.

"He told me to tell you . . . to take the three things— the three *necessities*—and to go as fast as you can . . . to the man from the east . . . to wait there . . . and if Apollonius doesn't come by sunset that you and the man are supposed to leave right away without him . . . and that it's a matter of life . . . of life . . . and . . . and . . ."

"Death?"

"Yes! Death!"

Myron certainly knew "the necessities." Apollonius had drilled the list into him from when he was a small child: in any emergency in which they had to leave town immediately, the necessary items to be taken were the modello, the tools, and the money, in that order of priority—the same items with which Apollonius had fled Alexandria twenty years ago when the monks were hunting him down.

"Attalus, if this is a joke I'm going to throw you in the river."

"It's not a joke, Myron! And Apollonius said that if you thought it was a joke, and that if you didn't do exactly what he says and right away, that he would put you in the hole again."

So it wasn't a joke—his master had certainly known how to communicate the seriousness of the matter. Attalus didn't know about the hole. But Myron couldn't go to the envoy now, no matter what problem Apollonius imagined he was having. Sira was going to meet him at the fountain at midnight.

"You said he's at the fountain now?"

"Yes, but you're not supposed to go there, Myron! There are soldiers there. They almost got me!"

"Soldiers . . ." Myron smirked. He had dealt with soldiers before. He found them to be self-important, puffed-up brutes, for the most part, always waving their swords around and spouting off about this law or that.

You couldn't make fun of the emperor, you couldn't tease the monks—one of Myron's friends had been flogged for waving a roasted goat leg beneath the noses of the half-starved ascetics. There was no law against taunting monks, but it seemed the soldiers like to make up extra rules when it suited them. Most of them were too stupid to know when they were being insulted in turn, and with their armor, they were amusingly slow. A soldier had given him a good cuffing once, when he had been caught off guard, but he wasn't afraid of soldiers.

There was no way he was going to abandon Apollonius, regardless, if his master was in any kind of trouble. He found himself almost insulted that Apollonius could think he wasn't more loved than that.

"Come on, Attalus—unless you're afraid."

"I'm not afraid," Attalus said, fearfully.

Hammurabi struggled to his feet and tried to come with them. Myron had to tell him three times to stay home.

Eight

Given on the eleventh day before the kalends of March at Milan in the year of the eighth consulship of Constantius Augustus and the consulship of Julian Caesar: If any persons should be proved to devote their attention to sacrifices or to worship images, We command that they shall be subjected to capital punishment. . . .

The crushed lotus drifted beneath the waterspout of one of the elephants' trunks. It went under, not to resurface.

As the prefect droned on from his codex, Apollonius took the measure of the situation, noting the number of soldiers, their positions, their weaponry—

Given on the sixth day before the ides of November at Constantinople in the year of the second consulship of Arcadius Augustus and the consulship of Rufinus: If any person should venerate images made by the work of mortals and destined to suffer the ravages of time, or should attempt to honor vain images with the offering of a gift, which even though it is humble, still is a complete outrage against religion . . .

Apollonius scanned the faces of his neighbors, most of whom had attended the feast celebrating the completion of the fountain. Many of them had made a point of personally complimenting and thanking the sculptor with enthusiasm and heartfelt sincerity for having contributed such wondrous loveliness and inspiring beauty to their town. How many would now stand in his defense? As he looked to each face, looking to catch the eyes of the men particularly, not one of them failed to look away, or to the ground, or to the horizon, or to the prefect or the bishop.

He could only hope that Myron would follow orders and not come, that his dear boy would take the modello and escape to the East to live on, to create another day.

> *Given on the sixth day before the kalends of March at Milan in the year of the consulship of Tatianus and Symmachus: No person shall approach the shrines, shall wander through the temples, or revere the images formed by mortal labor, lest he become guilty by divine and human laws. . . .*

He turned and looked up to his Kheimon.

At least I knew you, my dear. . . .

As he contemplated her uplifted countenance and her clear, forward gaze, the sights and sounds around him faded until he was alone with her again.

Physically, they had never been more intimate than when he held her in his arms that night above Thebes, but at least their minds and souls had met, if briefly. He drank deeply of her, treasuring yet another moment.

You were the best, my love, the best of Man—and a Woman, no less. . . .

The image he had created was of her physical and spiritual likeness, yet it was both more than her and less: it was the essence of the woman, what he saw and treasured in her, what he had always hoped that she could see in herself but seemed ever struggling against. His own longings and aspirations were there too: it was her, through him.

I know, I know—there's still the most important thing. . . . No, don't worry, my love. I've trained the boy well, and he's beginning to understand, I think—better probably than I. He is young yet, it is true, but he's a prodigy, a genius. Someday, in a place far away from here, he will be the one to create it, the image worthy of our reverence, the one whom even you could look up to. . . . I'm sorry you won't get to see it. I was meaning to put it right over there—

"Apollonius of Alexandria—" Peter was addressing him, the prefect having finished the reading of the law— "Do you confess, in contradiction to the law of God and man, that you have made this image and that you set it up in this place, an abomination to God and a temptation in the eyes of these blessed believers, that you have placed gifts before this false god, and that you have worshipped this graven image?"

"A false god?" Apollonius laughed. "She was *Anthropos*, Peter, of the same race as you and I, though in truth, she was far more woman than you were ever man—"

A flash blinded his left eye as one of the soldiers cuffed him hard across the face, knocking him to his knees.

"You will address the man of God as *Your Holiness* and with respect, old fool."

Peter waited for Apollonius to recover his senses and regain his feet before continuing evenly. "She was a mere woman—a mortal. That was well proven, was it not, Apollonius? And thus all the more disgraceful, that a base, mortal, imperfect creature should be so elevated and sanctified. It is only the immortal and perfect Lord our God who has the power, through his grace and forgiveness, to raise humanity up from the dust, from our low and sinful nature. But *you*, proud man, you dare put yourself in the position of God, taking the dust of the earth and forming it into the shape of an Eve and imagining her to be an innocent being, pure and without fault or sin. Only God and his son, Jesus, are sinless and eternal, Apollonius, and it is only by his grace that those who prostrate themselves before him in humility will live with him in eternity. As God's son was born to die and to be raised again, this pagan witch who was once struck down and has now been raised up by you will presently be struck down again, for thus said the Lord, *'Dust thou art, and unto dust shalt thou return.'*"

"Oh, it was your God who struck her down then?" Apollonius shook his head in disgust. "You deny, Peter, that it was you and your tribe of filthy monks who accomplished that courageous feat? So who was playing God then, Peter? What cowards—three dozen men against one woman—"

The soldier hit him across the back of the head so hard that Apollonius found himself face down on the paving stones, blood and dust filling in his mouth. He worked his way back up to his knees and spit out the pieces of teeth. As he struggled to his feet, unbalanced, no assistance was offered to him. The soldier drew back to strike again, but Peter interrupted with an upraised hand—

"Let this man stand before the Lord's judgment."

After finding his balance, Apollonius lifted his eyes again, and what the bishop saw in them caused him to take a step back. Peter didn't know why the man standing before

110

him wasn't yet humbled and in fear for his life, but it was clear that he was not. When the old sculptor straightened to his full height, he was taller than the bishop, certainly stronger. And there was black hell in his eyes.

Peter cleared his throat and defaulted to his favorite and most effective weapon—the quoting of biblical scripture, calling upon the very Word of God, which he hurled at Apollonius across the short distance between them.

"The eyes of the arrogant man will be humbled and the pride of men brought low; the LORD alone will be exalted in that day."

The man standing before him was untouched, unswayed.

"Pride goes before destruction, thou sinner, and a haughty spirit before a fall."

Apollonius continued to burn a hole through the bishop's soul.

But Peter wasn't finished. A pained, exquisite joy rose in his eyes, like the dark flood waters with which God in his anger was had once covered the earth and killed every man, woman and child, except for a handful on a boat. Peter had learned to welcome pain and suffering, having lived for years alone in the desert in a dugout with no windows and no door over its opening. He had learned to endure, with thankfulness, the agony of the freezing nights and the thirst of the days' boiling heat. He had embraced the weakness and the unending gnawing of hunger, the suffering of the body, in emulation and glorification of the pain his Lord had suffered.

"Yes, Apollonius, one blessed day, God rewarded his servant's humility and penitence with the commission of delivering his justice upon the wicked, so that it would be a sign to unbelievers . . ." Watching the old sculptor's eyes, he reached into the neckline of his robe, while quietly, cuttingly, offering a final scripture:

"The pride of your heart has deceived you, you who live in the clefts of the rocks and make your home on the heights, you who say to yourself, 'Who can bring me down to the ground?'"

Hanging from the frayed cord around his neck was the object that had rested next to his heart for twenty years.

"This would be my treasured and only possession, Apollonius, but as with all things on earth, it belongs not to me but to God above. One day, our good Lord lent it to me as a tool, and now it remains with me as a token that, in his mercy, he blessed his servant to be his hands, to help cleanse of the earth of Man's hubris and wickedness."

The talisman hanging from the cord wasn't a cross, but a shard of broken clay tile, its jagged edges stained a mottled dark brown.

∞

Of the events in Alexandria concerning the woman Hypatia, it was written by the historian Socrates Scholasticus:

> *Some of the monks, therefore, had hurried away with a fierce and bigoted zeal, and their ringleader was a reader named Peter. They waylaid her as she returned home, and dragging her from her chariot, they took her to the church called Caesareum, where they completely stripped her, and murdered her by scraping her skin off with tiles and bits of shell. After tearing her body in pieces, they took her mangled limbs to a place called Cinaron, and there, burnt them.*

Nine

MYRON AND ATTALUS ARRIVED at the square to find the crowd in a frenzy. The carpenter Ioannes, wielding his hammer, was clambering to reach the upper level of the fountain, pushed aloft by three of his neighbors. Two of the elephants' trunks and several of the antelopes' heads had already been broken off. A large woman was hanging off of a third trunk, hoisting her fat legs out of the water so as to bring her full weight to bear on the appendage. On the upper rim, a young man was straddling one of the reclining girls, bashing at her face and breasts with a large stone.

Myron saw his master standing silently, watching, a soldier holding each of his arms. In front of him stood the prefect, clutching a closed book, and a bald man in an ecclesiastical robe, hands raised heavenward in prayer. Many in the crowd were shouting curses while others stood by quietly, holding their children. Some of the men and most of the boys had scattered about the square, pulling at the edges of the paving stones, finding chunks that could be prised loose. A rock flew through the air in Apollonius's direction but hit the shoulder of one of the soldiers. He cursed and pointed his short sword in the general direction of the culprit.

Myron was stunned, rooted to the ground, unable to move his feet, unable to make sense of the scene before him.

The carpenter, having attained the top tier, was hefting his hammer, eyeing the figure above. Of a sudden, Apollonius flew forward, escaping the soldiers' grasp when they least suspected. Drawing a chisel from the inner band of his belt, he lunged toward the bishop. A grab at the sculptor's sleeve by one of the monks impeded his aim just enough that the chisel's arc, rather than slicing cleanly through the bishop's neck, cut a gash from his shoulder and down across his chest, severing the cord that held the tile shard. The shard arced high through the air and fell to the pavement, shattering into small pieces.

Before Apollonius could make a second thrust, a soldier and a monk were on him. The soldier died instantly when the chisel pierced his heart. The monk suffered a deep slash through his abdomen and fell to the ground writhing, clutching at his exposed intestines. In an instant, Apollonius was up and against the fountain's rim.

The mounted soldiers in the rear charged through the crowd towards him. Turning away from them, he climbed over the rim and splashed toward the men who had hoisted the carpenter aloft—but before he could reach them, a soldier intercepted him with a sword strike, chopping down on his left clavicle, rendering his one arm useless. He switched the chisel to his other hand and, with a sweeping kick, knocked the soldier's feet out from under him. Falling on the man, he held his head underwater, but had to rise to face three more soldiers who were wading through the fountain toward him, swords drawn.

Myron heard himself scream—"*No!*" His legs carried him forward.

The soldiers slowed as they advanced on their target. Apollonius awaited, chisel at the ready, his back to one of the fountain's columns. Four more joined the semicircle of those facing him. He rotated, sizing up each in turn. The odds were overwhelming, his position untenable.

He relaxed his shoulders and stood tall. Turning his back on them, he looked up to his lady above and, touching his fingers to his lips, raised his hand in a final salute.

When he turned again, he bellowed a curse at the bloodied, bewildered bishop, then laughed a grand laugh and charged into the forces allied against him.

ରେ

Myron was running at full tilt toward where his master had disappeared beneath a surge of slashing steel. Ahead in the crowd, one of the sisters who had danced with him at the feast was pointing at him, gesturing to one of the mounted soldiers. The baker's wife, next to her, confirmed to the soldier what the girl was saying. The soldier wheeled his horse and nudged it into a trot toward Myron, motioning for a second horseman to join him.

"They're going to kill you, Myron!" Attalus had caught up with him and was tugging frantically at his sleeve. Myron slowed to a walk.

He shrugged off Attalus' grasp but stopped and stood for a moment. He was halfway between the advancing horsemen and the edge of the square behind him. The soldiers were nudging their mounts into a slow gallop, separating along lines that would soon find Myron caught between them. All of the stories and lessons that his master had tried so hard to get into Myron's head were coalescing into meaningful lucidity.

Apollonius had risen once again above the melee, swinging one of the soldier's swords. He killed two more of them before being cut down, not to rise again.

Myron fought to control his emotions. He had to think. There was nothing he could do to save his master, but while he wasn't the blood-son of the man from Alexandria, the spirit of Apollonius surged through his veins, and as he watched his favorite thing, his most beloved thing, die, he knew what he needed to know about the modello, about what it meant to him, about himself and his love for the man who had raised him. In that moment, he determined to do what was necessary to carry on the mission, the mission that had become his own: he wanted nothing more than to live, to live to immortalize in stone the spirit of the greatest man he had ever known.

Myron never would have prostrated himself before his master during his lifetime—and his master would never have permitted him to do so—but as Apollonius breathed his last breaths, it seemed only right for Myron to drop to a knee and bow his head, particularly in that the act was timed perfectly to cause the horsemen to miss grabbing him as they thundered past and above.

Attalus was less fortunate. The boy tried to shield himself behind Myron, but one of the soldiers' legs caught his shoulder and sent him flying to land beneath the rear hooves of the other's horse. When his trampled body stopped rolling, it lay motionless. From the crowd, a woman screamed.

Myron leapt to his feet and wheeled to face the horsemen as they turned. He picked up a stone and threw it as hard and straight as he could, hitting one of them squarely in the face. The soldier recoiled, pulling up on the reins, causing his horse to rear and throw him to the pavement. The other soldier spurred and charged. Rather than trying to dodge him, Myron crouched and leapt, grabbing the bridle while swinging his legs up to wrap around the horse's neck. Pulling down and back on the bit with all his strength, he collapsed the animal's front legs, sending its rear into the air and its rider over the top. Myron rolled away just in time to save himself from being crushed by the tumbling mass.

But now more horsemen were riding hard toward him, followed by a good part of the enraged mob, their faces contorted in righteous fury. He recognized most of the people, but he no longer knew any of them.

He fled into the closest alley. The horseman in the lead followed him in at full gallop, the animal's breath hot on the back of his neck as they neared the alley's blocked end. He jumped to scramble over the wall ahead, the soldier's sword slashing at his legs—but the steel found only stone.

The street beyond was empty.

There was no time for taking the back alleys. He ran the shortest route to the workshop, where he stopped at the door, his heart pounding. The mob's shouts and the hammering of the horses' hooves were only a street or two away. Fighting the urge to run straight for the town's east gate to take refuge with the envoy, he dashed into the shop to snatch the modello off the shelf and throw a handful of tools into a bag. Atop these, he laid, more gently, Apollonius's monogrammed mallet. From the hole he retrieved one of the purses of coin, leaving the rest so as not to weigh himself down more than necessary. The bag was heavy but manageable. He checked the pouch on his belt—the spoon from Sira was still there. Her sash was still tied around his arm.

It was enough. He was ready.

He tried to make Hammurabi stay, but the dog wouldn't leave his side.

"Come on then, boy."

With the bag in hand, he ran out to the street, only to see, turning the corner toward him, two of the horsemen. Retreating into the shop, he barred the door and ran out through the back, shifting the bag so that he could pat the Parian marble one last time as he ran by.

Taking the back alley north, he had run most of its length before a soldier appeared at the end, blocking his path. At the south end, the butcher was standing, feet spread, wielding his cleaver.

He retreated through the yard and back into the shop, calling for Hammurabi to hurry inside. Laying the bag aside, he closed the door, barred it and leaned against it, the modello cradled in his arms.

⚬⚬

News of the violence had reached the market. Sira couldn't quite make out what was being said in the street—but when she heard the words "destroying" and "fountain" in the same breath, she dropped the wool she was folding and started to run, her mother calling after her.

By the time she arrived at the square, most of the mob had gone, but evidence of mayhem was everywhere.

A young woman was kneeling on the ground, wailing and pleading inconsolably, rocking a child's limp, broken body in her arms. Next to the fountain lay a dead soldier and a dying monk. Rocks and chunks of paving stone were strewn about the square, intermixed with trampled scarves, a soiled, twisted toga and orphaned sandals. Near the bodies, dark puddles had pooled. Spattered arcs of blood drops were already drying in the sun's heat. The water in the fountain's lower pool was crimson, the marble rim blotched and stained. The white lily she had left only two days before had been crushed beneath a bloody footprint. In the water, amidst the bodies of soldiers, floated a white-haired man, face down.

Men and boys were climbing about the fountain, working methodically at destroying what remained of the human figures and animals while two soldiers stood guard nearby. On the top tier, the central figure's arms had already been broken off. From a ladder leaned against her, a man was hacking at her elegant neck with a dull ax.

Sira screamed at him to stop. The man glanced in her direction but continued. After a few blows more, the head tumbled off and hit the stone below, rolling between the broken figures of the boys, bouncing down the steps and into the mid-tier pool. A teenager picked it up and held it aloft, his trophy raising a cheer from those below. He tossed it over the rim. It landed in the lower pool next to Sira, splashing blood and water across her face and tunica.

She leapt over the rim, ignoring the shouts of the soldiers, and lifted the head out of the water, struggling with the weight. Part of the nose and one of the ears were broken off. The chin was damaged. Cradling it in her arms, she climbed out and, in a daze, began walking in the direction of the sculptor's shop, her fingers unconsciously caressing the sculpted hair. No one tried to stop her.

CR

When she arrived, the street on which the shop stood was crowded with people craning to see what they could of the commotion at the front. The soldiers were attempting to maintain order while the mob shouted demands and hurled rocks at the shop's door and shuttered windows. The bishop and the prefect stood nearby, arguing heatedly. The front of the bishop's robe was torn, his chest and shoulder wrapped in blood-soaked bandages.

Sira couldn't push through the throng. Backtracking to a side street, she made her way to the shop's back alley, only to find it guarded by soldiers.

She retraced her steps to the front. She wouldn't be able to carry the heavy head much further.

A man emerged from a house across the street with a piece of burning wood from a cooking fire, and before the soldiers could stop him, with the immediate neighbors yelling in protest from their windows, he hurled the torch high into the air, onto the shop's thatched roof, where it began to smolder. There was a frenzied effort to find and raise ladders to reach the fire before it spread, but the flames rose quickly. Within minutes, smoke began pouring from the eaves of the second level.

Sira, abandoning all manners, pushed her way roughly through the crowd to as close to the front door as she was able. One of the church elders shoved her back and out of the way.

A decision had been reached. The bishop crossed his arms. The prefect issued an order. Four of the soldiers approached the shop's entry with a large timber and began battering the door repeatedly, splintering and cracking the wood until only a few pieces dangled from the hinges. Smoke wafted from the top of the exposed opening.

Sira, praying Myron wasn't inside, worked her way around to see through the doorway. The room inside appeared just as it had when she had first seen Myron working there, splitting the stone.

Then she saw him. Her blue silk sash was tied around the lower half of his face, protecting him from the smoke. Cradled in one of his arms was a bronze figurine. He opened the back door, determined to escape the smoke and fire, but on seeing the soldiers in the yard, he closed and barred it again. The draft of new air from the back sent more smoke and flames billowing through the front entrance.

The crowd began chanting, "Burn, pagan, burn! Burn, sinner, burn!"

Sira's father appeared at her side. He nudged her with his elbow, grinning, wanting to know what was going on, excited by the excitement. She turned away from him. On the keystone above the entryway was the engraving of the lady whose head she now held in her hands. The image that had helped her find her beloved was blackening from the smoke.

A large soldier who, judging by the open gash beneath his eye, had recently been hit in the face by something, dismounted from his horse. Dunking his cloak in a nearby water trough, he covered his head and shoulders with it and, to the shouted encouragement of his comrades, charged determinedly through the fiery entrance. Many in the crowd cheered. Others, preferring to see the boy burn, booed. Inside, a furious barking and growling went up, followed by a terrible yelping and silence. A hush fell as the flames crept down the frame of the doorway and pushed through the shutters of the lower windows. Then came sounds of crashing furnishings, bursting pottery and smashing stone. And silence again. A bloodcurdling, high-pitched scream reached the street—followed by the soldier, clutching madly at his face, stumbling blindly against the fiery walls of the entranceway. He spun out into the street, his hair and clothing ablaze, and pitched face down on the pavement. His comrades rushed to him and struggled to beat and smother the fire with their cloaks. But by the time the flames were extinguished and the man was turned face up, his blackened body no longer moved.

The soldiers stepped back in horror. From the socket of the man's left eye protruded the bowl of a bronze spoon, its handle lodged deep in the man's brain.

Sira watched the shop entrance. A burning timber fell across the doorway, partially blocking it. When a draft parted the smoke, she saw her Myron, still inside but alive. His tunica was torn, his lip bleeding. The knotted sash of blue silk had fallen down around his neck. He was retrieving the modello from the workbench, where he must have left it during the fight. As he took the sculpture into the crook of his arm again, he looked up and saw her through the doorway.

He waved to her. She waved back. Untying the sash, he pulled it from around his neck, touched it to his lips and raised it in a solemn salute.

Another burning timber crashed down between them. The flames and smoke engulfed the doorway until he could no longer be seen.

The Christians crossed themselves. The pagans uttered quiet oaths. The Jews, watching from the back of the crowd, slipped away, muttering prayers.

The head of the sculpture was too heavy for Sira to hold. Her own body seemed too heavy to hold erect any longer. She turned to her father and put the head in his hands, but just as he was taking it, he noticed the bishop watching them intently. In feigned anger and disapproval, her father took the head and dashed it to the street, shattering it into pieces.

The old woman to whom Sira had offered the coin, with the mark of the cross on her forehead, hobbled forward and spat on the remains of the face. Her spittle trickled from the sculpture's eye, down its marble cheek. The woman crossed herself and flashed Sira a toothless, spiteful grin.

Sira looked from the pieces on the ground to her father, from her father to the bishop, from the bishop to the satisfied faces in the crowd around her. This was not her world.

Before anyone could stop her, she ran for the doorway and, gathering speed, leapt over the fallen timber and into the curtain of fire.

Coming soon . . .

Part II

A New Eden

One

IT WAS MARIA'S FOURTH WEEK on the job, and the third week during which when she knocked on the door of Suite 117 and called out "housekeeping," there was no reply. Using her passkey, she entered, pulled the cart in behind her and quietly shut the door.

The suite featured a kitchenette, a large Jacuzzi tub, and gas fireplaces in both the bedroom and living area. The Prairie-influenced design, in light woods and local stone, was finished in a warm palette, with sensuous fabrics covering the plush furnishings. Accenting the walls were sepia photo-prints of the local fauna. French doors opened onto a flagstone patio, beyond which a double terrace of flowering flora bordered a tidy square lawn, a cascading stone fountain in the corner. The perimeter of sculpted hedging, taller on the sides to provide privacy from the adjacent units, was cropped shorter across the end to allow a sweeping southerly view of the high-desert valley below. The rugged range of snowcapped mountains rising close to the west and the soft rolling hills to the east cradled the city below, stretching away to the distant, hazy horizon.

On a lounge chair reclined on the patio, the suite's lone occupant lay prone in the sun, her head to the side, her eyes closed. She hadn't moved when the housekeeper entered. She was completely nude.

Maria cleared away the breakfast tray from room service, wiped down the slate-floored bathroom, replenished the towels and toiletries and emptied the nearly empty wastebaskets. She tucked the tip left on the bed into the pocket of her apron. As she stripped the Egyptian-cotton sheets, her eyes were drawn again to the patio.

The young woman was hardly older than Maria herself, probably in her mid-twenties. Her lithe, runner's body was already well tanned, her bobbed chestnut hair gleaming in the sun. She had been present in the suite each day Maria had entered to clean, usually on the patio reading a book or writing longhand in a spiral-bound journal. Her face was pretty, in a tomboyish way, with a girlish cuteness that had annealed with experience to a tauter set of the mouth; her moss-green eyes tracked in a gazelle-like watchfulness, not afraid, but ever mindful, ready. When she wasn't sleeping or sunning she might acknowledge the maid's presence with a polite nod, but otherwise she said nothing and made no requests. The dozen or so books she had finished reading during her stay were mostly paperback suspense novels and biographies. Some days, Maria would find her standing silently at the end of the lawn in a bathrobe, gazing in silence at the valley.

The suite was always quiet. The televisions and radio were never on. A leather satchel, in which a notebook computer and camera case were tucked, had been left leaning against the wardrobe. Maria never saw the computer or camera being used, or a phone, if the woman had one. Surely she had one. Hanging in the closet next to the bathroom were three outfits of casual travel wear. Next to the single piece of generic carry-on luggage was a pair of well-used but clean walking shoes and a pair of sandals.

In the three weeks the guest had occupied the suite, none of the other staff had seen her leave the suite either, save for over the last few evenings when she had gone down to the hotel lounge to sit at the bar, where she would order a cocktail and take her dinner with a glass of wine while continuing her reading. After dinner, she would always return directly to her suite for the night.

The woman intrigued Maria, so much so that her thoughts were filled with her night and day.

One afternoon when the woman was sunning on the patio, she began talking in her sleep. To Maria it sounded as if she were arguing with someone, and in increasingly desperate tones, but in a language Maria didn't at all recognize. Then, with a sharp turn of her head, as though someone had slapped her, she fell silent again.

Who *was* she? How could she afford to stay in such an expensive place for weeks on end, and if she were wealthy enough to do so, where was the rest of her luggage? Where was the expensive clothing and jewelry? Didn't she have friends or family, or an employer she needed to check in with occasionally? Maybe she wasn't rich at all. Maybe the owners of the resort were letting her stay, helping her through a difficult situation of some kind. Maybe she was recovering from a broken heart. Could she be hiding from someone? Had she killed an abusive husband and escaped with his money? Maybe she had been the secret love interest of a handsome, rich landowner in Mexico until discovering he was already married—just like in the telenovelas—or maybe she was a foreign spy between assignments, awaiting instructions before jetting off to another exotic destination to seduce and poison a diplomat who had learned too much. Despite the careful way about her, the woman seemed entirely sure of herself. Maria wondered if there was a small pistol in the handbag. She hoped so.

Presently her eyes wandered again to the woman's body, coming to rest on the dimpled hollows at the top of the firmly mounded, athletic buttocks. She reached around her own waist to touch the base of her own back, wondering if she looked the same there: they had similar builds, similar frames. But Maria had never seen her own naked backside. She certainly would never lounge about in the nude. It was a marvel to her that any woman could be so comfortable allowing a stranger to see her that way. She herself would have been much too ashamed—it was the way she was raised, she supposed.

The woman opened her eyes. She was staring directly at Maria, studying her with a piercing intensity.

Maria flushed. Fighting her reflex to look away, she stood straighter, taller, feeling naked herself under a scrutiny that seemed to see through her clothes, through the fabric of her very thoughts—but she had nothing to hide. Nothing. Finally, the stare softened into what appeared to be a pained melancholy, as if Maria perhaps reminded her of someone. The woman smiled faintly, almost apologetically, and rolled over languidly to expose her front to the sun. By the time she closed her eyes again, the smile was gone.

Maria hurriedly finished making the bed, her heart racing. She gave a final fluff to the pillows and wheeled the cart out of the room, her thoughts still tumbling. Before closing the door, she stole a last, lingering look.

She was pushing the cart down the hall toward the next suite when she recalled that she hadn't been to confession in months. She wasn't sure when she would go again, but she was sure that when she did—if she did—she wouldn't tell the priest about the woman in Suite 117. There were just some things a girl wanted to keep for herself.

ॐ

The world outside was visible only through the mesh screen covering the face of the sweltering black burqa. She was struggling to work her way through a crowd of thick-bearded men and wild-eyed boys who were shouting and gesticulating in righteous anger, many with stones in their hands as they pushed forward for a clear shot at their target, a short, writhing object set in a clearing in the mob's midst. At first impression, the living thing appeared to be a stunted animal with no legs—but no, it was a fully formed teenage girl, buried to her waist, her legs encased beneath the ground, her hands and arms bound tightly about her exposed torso. A thin sheet had been tied around the exposed top half of her body, but the cloth had been partially ripped away by the sharp stones and the girl's struggles. Blood poured from gashes on her face, head and shoulders. The side of her skull was already partially caved where a large rock had smashed against it, an eye hanging partially out of its socket, the cheek beneath the eye torn through from mouth to jaw. The girl was wailing, pleading for mercy as she weaved and ducked vainly to dodge the hurled missiles. But the stones continued to land, in dull, unremitting thuds against her clothing and hair, in wet smacks against her skin and bones.

There was no way to reach the girl, no matter how hard she tried. Despite her efforts, she couldn't force her way through the men. They pushed her back roughly, threatening her with the same fate as the girl's if she persisted. She tried to speak, to scream, to beg them to stop and let her help the girl, but no sound would come out of her mouth. The other women of the village were standing well back, their black, shapeless forms clustered on the street corners and in the darkened doorways. Not one would come to the girl's assistance.

Suddenly the crowd dispersed.

The victim was motionless, her eyes still open, a slumped, human gravestone tilted askew in a field of strewn rocks and bloodied chunks of concrete.

She ran and knelt next to the silent body, cradling death in her arms, rocking the girl, trying to shush away the cries of confusion and terror that lingered in the air, sounds she could still hear in the silence and would always hear, sounds the girl would never make again.

"Shh . . . shh . . . it's over now, it's all over . . . it's okay now . . ."

But then there was more screaming in the distance, and she got up and ran toward the girls' school, as she always did. The school was on fire, as it always was, surrounded by the cordon of religious enforcers who held the hysterical, pleading mothers at bay, proclaiming censoriously that the girls' heads were not properly covered, that they couldn't be allowed to exit, they couldn't be allowed to be seen in public in such a state—the law stated it clearly. A man standing nearby shouted angrily that the girls were not supposed to be going to school regardless, that they properly belonged at home, that the fire was Allah's punishment for the sin of seeking knowledge instead of obedience. The girls pressed desperately against the padlocked gates and windows, screaming to be let out as the smoke and flames took them one by one.

She pushed through the cordon and ran to the gate where she tugged, tore and twisted at the gate's padlocked chain with her bare hands, an enforcer on horseback bearing down on her from behind. The girls begged her, clutching at the sleeves of her burqa through the gate, screaming as the flames grew unbearably hot and the scorching *chain blistered her hands. She could hear the steaming, snorting breath of the horse behind her as she begged for someone, anyone, to help—but there was no one, no one to stop the evil, no one to stop the horror, the injustice, the insanity. . . .*

She awoke in a panic, her eyes flickering open, squinting at the hot orb above. Anxiously, without moving, she closed them again, trying to remember where she was, what had happened to her, trying to identify, to assess—

My name is Paige Keller. I'm an American. I'm at a resort, on a hillside. The hill is on the north end of a valley, a valley in northeastern Nevada. I am safe here. I'm back in America—I'm no longer in danger. No longer in danger . . .

Yet the sound of the horse's wet snorting had been too real. She couldn't shake it. She focused on relaxing her mind, slowing her breathing.

How long had she slept? How long since the maid had left?

The frequency of the nightmares, which nearly always played out the same, had begun to abate somewhat. It had been four or five days since the last episode—but there they were again today, in the middle of the afternoon. She wondered if they would ever let her be, or if they would plague her for the rest of her life. The enforcer on horseback was a new element though—and she realized that her internal antenna, so acutely attuned to danger, was still crackling ominously.

She heard the horse's snorting again.

Without raising her head, she determined that the sound had come from the far end of the lawn. Feigning sleep still, she shifted her head slowly, just enough that she could see, between her lashes, the hedge at the lawn's end, while in her mind's eye she measured the distance to her purse in the nightstand by the bed.

A movement through the hedge's upper leaves revealed, beneath a black, round-rimmed parson's hat, the face of a young man. His eyes were dark. He had a short, squared-off beard with no mustache. To his left, visible through the leaves, was the head of his horse, shifting nervously. The man's eyes were flitting along Paige's naked body, his expression torn between lust and loathing.

Without covering herself, she sat up abruptly and stared back at him. The flash of guilt on his face settled into a sneer—he spurred his horse and rode away noisily.

She rose and walked unhurriedly back inside, locking the doors behind her. After showering under hot water, then cold, she sat on the bed and tried to read, but couldn't concentrate. Though the hedge was less than four feet high on the lawn side, the maintenance path running along the outside, lower on the slope of the hill, was a good nine feet below the hedge's crown. If the man had seen her by accident, he could have ridden on. But he hadn't. The fact that he hadn't ridden on wouldn't have bothered her so much except that, upon being caught, he hadn't shown even a modicum of appreciation for what he was seeing. His response had been quite the opposite. And there had been something else, something in the sanctimonious censure of his expression that reminded her too much of the behavior of other men in other places.

She shook it off. An hour earlier than usual, she dressed for dinner. To her customary, casual ensemble she added a pair of modest freshwater pearl earrings and a simple, matching neck chain, its single pearl resting at the base of her throat.

(to be continued . . .)

If you've enjoyed the story so far, please consider supporting the author's work by posting a short review on Amazon and/or on Goodreads.
Every review is greatly appreciated. Thank you!

To alert the author to any errors or typos in the text or to offer any comments, please email dobby@cordair.com or contact Quent Cordair via Facebook.

For the latest Cordair fiction and news, please visit the author's website at www.quentcordair.com or the author's Amazon page.

About the Author

BORN IN 1964 in southern Illinois, **QUENT CORDAIR** was raised in an insular, fundamentalist religious sect. In his childhood, he fell in love with books at the local library, a treasured gateway to the outside world. After an enlistment in the U.S. Marines, he launched his writing career. His first short story was published in 1991 by the Atlantean Press Review. Attempts to sell a second published story door to door failed. To support his writing, he waited tables, worked as a security guard, stocked groceries, and stuffed envelopes on the graveyard shift at a mail-processing center. But such employment left him too spiritually drained to write, so he sought work more in keeping with his esthetic interests. Having taught himself to paint, he began taking portrait commissions at his easel in a local park. After exhibiting in street fairs for two years, he opened his own art gallery in 1996. Today, Quent Cordair Fine Art, located in Napa, California, represents more than two dozen Romantic Realist painters and sculptors of international renown.

With the gallery now managed by his wife, Linda Cordair, the author's attentions are focused fully on his writing. Quent Cordair's acclaimed short stories, screenplays and novels are drawn from his lifetime of experience and interests in romance, adventure, individualism, religion, history, politics, philosophy and art. The Cordairs live in Napa with their cats, Lexie and Sadie, and their border collie, Mollie.

www.quentcordair.com

Printed in Great Britain
by Amazon.co.uk, Ltd.,
Marston Gate.